C000154500

OBSESSED

Ruchi Kokcha is a writer and a poet who truly believes in her saying, 'People come, people go, poetry stays.' A lover of stories, she did her master's in English literature from Delhi University. Currently working as a teacher, when not immersed in books or typing her heart out, she loves weight-training at the gym or swaying to a Bollywood dance number. *Obsessed* is her first novel.

OBSESSED
RUCHI KOKCHA

HARPER
BLACK
An Imprint of HarperCollins *Publishers*

First published in India in 2018 by Harper Black
An imprint of HarperCollins *Publishers*
A-75, Sector 57, Noida, Uttar Pradesh 201301, India
www.harpercollins.co.in

2 4 6 8 10 9 7 5 3 1

P-ISBN: 978-93-5277-917-8
E-ISBN: 978-93-5277-918-5

Typeset in 11/14 Minion Pro at
Manipal Digital Systems, Manipal

Printed and bound at
Thomson Press (India) Ltd

To Vagmi, the brighter side of my life.

1

What one sees in the world outside is often a reflection of the internal landscape of one's mind. There were no birds chirping on the still branches of the trees outside Avik's bedroom window. Green leaves were scattered over the brown welcome mat outside his door. No one could tell that there had been a storm the previous night amidst the silence that enveloped the street until one saw the aftermath.

Avik woke up feeling restless and noticed the chaos all around him in his one-bedroom ground-floor flat in Mumbai. The bedroom looked more like a laundry, thanks to Mumbai's rains. Two cords, heavy with clothes that refused to dry, were strung across the room, bisecting each other just below the fan. A heap of washed clothes lay on the beanbag, waiting to be ironed and placed in the wardrobe. In the laundry bag, the clothes waged a war against each other, fighting for space as the pile continuously grew day after day.

Avik frowned at the laundry on his way to the bathroom. He looked into the deep black eyes that stared back at him from the mirror as he brushed his teeth. Mumbai had sapped his vigour over time, like the sun evaporates a pond, little by little. He was thirty but looked older. Thanks to his busy schedule at work, he often skipped meals and had no time to exercise. Of average build, he could be called fit if he wore a loose t-shirt or a kurta, but his paunch was clearly visible in the shirt and pants he wore to office every day.

Avik showered quickly, wrapped himself in his cotton towel and rushed to the ironing board, on which he had laid out his favourite grey shirt and black trousers after ironing them last night in preparation for today's meeting. His utilitarian wardrobe was full of dark-coloured shirts and trousers that could bear the grime and soot of city life. It was the only effort he made to look smart.

The sight of the kitchen sink was obnoxious to him. He did not feel like cooking. There was neither the time nor the clean utensils to make breakfast, as the maid hadn't turned up in four days. He looked inside the stinking refrigerator, threw away half a loaf of stale bread and a bunch of foul-smelling vegetables and checked the expiry date on the milk carton. He gulped down milk straight from the carton, an easy option. The mess was getting on his nerves.

Making his way around his cluttered flat was difficult. Even more challenging was finding a matching pair of socks. His shoes were covered in sludge from the previous day's rains. There was no point in polishing them because of the water-logging problem in his neighbourhood, but he did it anyway. He combed his hair into the centre-parted style that he hadn't changed in ten years.

Avik locked the mess inside and took a few steps towards the porch, ready to leave for his office, when the beauty of the chaos outside gripped him. He took a deep breath, taking in the fragrance of faraway places that had blown in with the storm in an attempt to cleanse himself of the stench he had been subjected to inside.

It is after the most furious winds have passed that one can see life as it really is: total chaos, he thought. He felt the chaos reverberating within him as he walked briskly towards the main road, hoping to find a taxi soon.

His gait had been a little clumsy ever since the operation he had had in childhood to remove the extra digit on each foot. One noticed his slight limp only if one paid careful attention, but Mumbai was not a city that waited for anyone's heedfulness.

Avik did not want to be late for the meeting with Dheeraj Sahay, his boss, who had hinted the previous evening that an important assignment would be given to one of the journalists. Despite working at a reputed magazine for a long time, Avik was still waiting for his big break. He was desperate to earn this opportunity; he was sure it could change his life, given what Sahay had implied.

As he sat in the taxi on his way to work, he stared out of the window, watching the buildings flash past him, thinking about how he had left so much of his life behind in his struggle to become successful, to rise above the fight for bread, butter and a space in Mumbai's local trains, to enjoy the finer things in life. So much time had gone by without a taste of the success he was always waiting for. His life was comfortable in a mediocre way, but he desired much more than that.

Outside his office building he saw Sonia, his sexy colleague who was one of the leading contenders for the assignment. Sonia had moved to Mumbai from London three years ago after her divorce. An impetuous decision based on physical attraction had done her no good as far as nuptial bliss was concerned, but according to her, the failed marriage had taught her a valuable lesson. She now stayed away from emotional attachments but was a master of utilitarian friendships.

Avik knew that Sonia would go to any extent to snatch an opportunity she was interested in. She believed business was best conducted when devoid of ethics. Morality was something that pulled a person down.

He, on the other hand, believed himself incapable of stooping low for the sake of his job. His conscience was something he prized more than his career. It was for this reason that, despite being in the line for ten years, he had not made a significant mark, while it hadn't taken Sonia much time to be on a par with him. He wanted success, but on his own terms.

'Hey! All set for the meeting?' Sonia asked him as she sashayed towards the entrance to the office building in her black suede pumps.

'Yeah, sure.' Avik tried hard to hide his lack of assurance.

'Do you have any idea what the assignment that Sahay talked about yesterday is about?' he asked as they entered the elevator together.

'I have no clue, but sources say it's so huge that it can change the course of one's career,' she said in her half-baked British accent as she stepped out of the elevator and walked into the office.

Her words left him thinking. *This is the chance I have been waiting for since the beginning of my career. I have to make sure Sahay chooses me*, he thought as he swiped his access card and dashed inside.

Avik paced up and down the conference room while Sonia sipped her black coffee. Sahay was expected at any minute. Avik observed Sonia as she stood beside the window, examining her finely polished red nails. She wore a knee-length fitted black dress that accentuated her curves. Her Louis Vuitton purse hung from her left arm.

Why does she have to dress so sexily on important days like this? Avik thought. *It becomes so hard to divert Sahay's attention from her.*

Sonia finished her coffee and sat down. She gave Avik a pouty smile as she crossed her legs.

There she goes. What an attention seeker. She knows how desperate I am for this assignment. Her smile says it all. Avik forced himself to return her smile.

The wait was hard for him. He felt that the longer Sonia observed him, the more nervous he would appear to her. He sat on the chair right next to hers to avoid her hazel eyes that were submerged in make-up.

'How are you both doing?' Sahay said loudly as he came striding through the door.

Avik stood up and moved to the chair right next to the one Sahay took and opposite Sonia's.

'Are just the two of us in the running for this assignment?'Sonia asked Sahay in a sugar-sweet tone.

Sahay nodded. 'My best two.' He winked at her, irritating Avik.

'And what is it about?' Avik asked in an attempt to get Sahay's attention before Sonia stole it, as she always did.

'Brace yourself, guys. I want one of you to cover the story of Kalki Rajput's death,' Sahay declared, clearly excited.

Avik and Sonia exchanged sceptical glances.

'But this is such an old story. Why would anyone still be interested in it?' Sonia asked, tapping her nails on the table, having lost interest already.

'Yes, the story is six years old, but is it a complete story? No. Think about it. Every channel broadcast the news of her death, every journalist gave his or her perspective about the case, but no one was able to discover what actually happened, and till today it remains a riddle yet to be solved,' Sahay replied, sipping his tea.

'Have any additional facts come to light about the case?' Avik inquired, wanting to show Sahay that he was a better bet for the assignment than Sonia.

'No, all we have are some speculations.'

'Oh come on! How can we pursue a story with only speculations to go by?' Sonia demanded.

'What speculations?' Avik asked as he took out his pen and notebook to take notes.

'One, it might have been an accident, although I don't think it was. Two, Kalki committed suicide on finding out about her husband's extramarital affair. Three, Mr Rajput might have gotten her killed, for the same reason,' Sahay listed out the theories one by one.

'Was there any witness besides her daughter? Ananki Rajput was present at the scene, but she's been in an asylum ever since her mother's death,' Avik said.

'This is such a waste of time,' Sonia said as she got up to leave, upsetting Sahay.

'Sonia, are you giving up on this assignment so easily? Where is the tigress that does not hesitate to rip into a story?' Sahay asked, his voice rising.

'This story is a dead end. The only person who knows what happened is now insane. It isn't possible to get the truth from her,' Sonia said as she walked towards the door. She had lost the enthusiasm that had exuded from her earlier.

Avik, on the other hand, wasn't ready to give up.

'Sonia is right. We can't take Ananki's word for anything. Who would believe a madwoman's story?' he asked Sahay.

Sahay scratched his chin thoughtfully for a few minutes before smiling crookedly.

'In order to make people believe it, all we have to do is print it.' He guffawed.

Sonia gave Sahay a vexed look, opened the door and left the room. Sahay stood up and put his hand on Avik's shoulder, clearly waiting for a positive response from him.

'Let me think about it,' Avik looked at him and said.

'All right, take your time, but let me remind you, if you are able to successfully pursue this story, it will be the crowning jewel of your career. Keep in mind the fame, the status and the perks it will bring.'

Avik walked slowly to his cubicle, which was adjacent to Sonia's.

'Sonia.' Avik pulled his chair close to hers. 'What do you think about the story?' he asked softly.

'I already told you what I think about it. This assignment is doomed,' she replied as she touched up her make-up.

She put her make-up kit back in her bag and started checking her email, paying little attention to Avik.

'Should I go for it? Don't you think I have waited long enough?'

'I don't think it will bring you any success,' she replied, her eyes still fixed on her computer screen. 'Also, are you ready to move to Delhi for the sake of this story? Who knows when that mad bitch will bark. I am going to have a smoke, you coming?' Sonia said as she stood up.

'No, you carry on,' Avik replied, forcing a smile, although all he felt was desperation.

Avik had given little thought to the fact that he might have to shift to Delhi. Leaving Mumbai would mean leaving his world behind and returning to the pandemonium he had left a long time ago.

'How will I convince Trisha?' he murmured, loud enough for Sonia to overhear.

'Long-distance relationships never work,' she said as she pulled out her Louis Vuitton wallet, a lighter and a pack of cigarettes from her purse.

'We're going through a rough patch. Moving to Delhi would be the end of it,' Avik told Sonia.

'Of course it would. When a relationship is new, people make efforts. They take time out from busy schedules to spend time together. The actual test of a relationship comes after the waves of infatuation have ebbed. Other things take priority. The relationship can wait but a deadline won't. You better think twice before accepting the assignment,' Sonia said and left.

Avik left work early. He wanted to be away from the hustle-bustle of the office to think clearly, to calm the turmoil in his mind. There was only one place that could absorb all his negativity – Chowpatty, the sponge of Mumbai.

Avik took off his shoes, stood on the wet sand and looked around. He walked towards a bunch of kids playing football. He longed to join them, having almost forgotten the last time he had played any sport. The kids welcomed him to the game. After playing for an hour, he felt less stressed.

He waved goodbye to the kids and walked towards the sea. He sprawled on the sand, the incoming waves lapping around him, washing the dirt off his shirt. He lay there till he could feel the tide rising around him, submerging him, purging him of the uncertainties that battled in his mind.

Avik was clear about what he had to do. He dialled Sahay's number.

'I will leave for Delhi tomorrow, but I have a condition.'

'What is it?' Sahay asked.

'I will not stay with my mother. You will have to arrange accommodation for me.'

'Don't worry about it,' Sahay assured him and hung up.

Sahay walked up to Sonia, who was standing at the window in his office, and wrapped his arms around her from behind, his erection pressing into her.

'You are such a dog.' She giggled as he started to unzip her dress.

'I could never send you to Delhi, honey. What would I do without you?' he said as he turned her around, kissing her slender neck, pressing her ample bosom into his chest. 'Come on, show me that tattoo you got in Bangkok.'

'Tattoo? What tattoo?' Sonia pushed him away, feigning ignorance.

'Darling, the entire office knows what you did on that official trip to Bangkok, thanks to the two idiots who accompanied you.'

The previous month, Sonia, along with two of her juniors, Prashant and Nysa, had gone to Bangkok to cover a conference. On the last night, the three of them had gone out and gotten quite drunk and as they were walking down the streets, Sonia had caught sight of a tattoo parlour. She had insisted on going in and getting a tattoo. She had chosen to get a little sword, right next to her crotch.

Prashant and Nysa were embarrassed when Sonia had walked out of the changing room in a robe that she had forgotten to tie shut. She was naked from the waist down it. The tattoo artist had made her sit on a reclining chair, with her legs spread so he could work on her. When he had started to ink her, Sonia could not help but cry out. Her cries had been a mixture of pain and pleasure, shouts followed by moans that had made Prashant hard; he hadn't been able to take his eyes off her for even a second. Almost all of her eye make-up had been washed away by tears by the time the tattoo was done.

Sahay did not let her go till he had seen the sword in all its glory.

Avik called Trisha on his way back home. He wanted to meet her and tell her about the decision he had taken.

'Can we meet?' he asked as soon as she picked up.

'Avik, not today. I am really tired and need to sleep. I woke up at 5 in the morning to work on a presentation and have not had a minute's rest. Is it important?'

'It is important, maybe not for you but for me.' Avik was piqued by her reply.

'Can you not wait till tomorrow? I have to deliver a presentation, after that I can meet you for lunch or coffee.'

'It can't wait till tomorrow. It's urgent,' Avik said, emphasizing the last part.

'Okay, tell me over the phone,' Trisha insisted.

'I can't tell you over the phone. Can you not spare just ten minutes for me from your busy schedule?' he almost shouted.

'I can, but not today. I said I would meet you tomorrow,' she yelled back.

'Your tomorrow never arrives. It's either now or never. You decide,' Avik said and hung up.

Trisha called him back immediately.

'Fine. But only for half an hour,' she said.

'Okay, I will pick you up in ten minutes.'

Trisha could not understand Avik's urgency. *We spoke last night and he was fine. What has happened to him all of a sudden?* she wondered.

Trisha was twenty-nine. She was a strong, independent woman and had been working in advertising for the past seven years. She was passionate about her work. It was what had attracted Avik to her in the first place. But over time, their relationship had taken a back seat, for which both of them were to be blamed equally.

Perhaps he has succumbed to his mother's wishes and decided to marry a girl of her choice, a simple girl who can look after her son, not like a wife but like a mother. I can never be the daughter-in-law she wants. Moreover, I don't plan to be someone's daughter-in-law right now. We talked about this and he was fine with it. Has he changed his mind now under her influence? she wondered as she washed her round face, looked in the mirror, combed her short, stylishly cut hair and applied lip gloss on her thin pink lips.

Avik gave her a missed call. It was time to meet him and clear the clouds of doubt that hovered over their relationship. She rushed downstairs. She hugged him as if she had not seen him in ages, knowing something bad was about to come. She looked at him with dark, unblinking eyes.

'Not here,' he said almost in a whisper, avoiding her fervent gaze.

Her eyes had always been one of the greatest sources of inspiration for him. He could see himself in them with crystal clarity.

Trisha was not a woman who would agree to everything that her man said or believed. She corrected him when she thought he was wrong, guided him when he needed help, encouraged him during times of despair and appreciated him when he met with success.

She sat behind him on his bike and held him tightly. Somehow she felt her grip on him loosening.

Is this a bad sign? She hoped not.

She squeezed her eyes shut in an attempt to block out her negative thoughts and focus on something positive.

She remembered their first meeting at Shameet's birthday party. Both had been hiding themselves in their respective corners. But she had spotted him. Not quite tall and with a slim build, he looked fit. If one judged him on a purely physical scale he would not score more than average, but there was something in his eyes that added a magnetic charm to his personality.

Wow! What eyes! Black and large. They look dewy, not because of the smoke in the room but probably because they mirror a warm heart, she had thought as she stared at him.

She had kept her gaze fixed on him while he stood by a window, looking out as if in search of something.

Just when she was beginning to feel that this philosopher might never snap out of his thoughts and was about to leave, he had turned towards her. She had given him a smile, to which he had reacted in a rather surprised manner. It was hard for him to believe that an attractive woman would approach him.

She had walked up to him and they had decided to move out of the smoke-filled room to find some fresh air. Soon, they were engrossed in conversation and did not even realize when the last of the guests left. It was 4.30 in the morning. Trisha had wanted to call a taxi, but Avik had insisted on dropping her home on his bike.

Reminiscing about their first meeting helped calm her. She was ready to talk to him now.

He stopped in front of their favourite coffee shop, a place he thought would be perfect for closure. He ordered her a cappuccino but she was least interested in it. He sat down opposite her, grappling with what to say. He looked into her pitch-dark eyes. They were full of questions and he realized that he could no longer put off the inevitable.

'I'm moving to Delhi for an assignment. I do not know for how long,' he blurted out, startling her.

She stared at him.

His attention was focused on her face, as he wanted to read her expressions rather than listen to what she had to say. He had always trusted body language more than words.

She forced a smile and took a sip of the coffee that had turned cold in the silence that had passed between them at the table.

'So what is the assignment? It must be big enough for you to move,' she finally said.

'Yes. I am going to cover the story of Kalki Rajput's death. No one knows what actually happened except her daughter Ananki. The one—'

'The one who has been in an asylum for the last six years,' Trisha completed his sentence. 'Are you totally out of your mind, Avik? Do you have any idea what you are up to?' She was furious. She would never have stopped him from moving ahead in his career, being ambitious herself, but this move, she felt, would exterminate his career, if not him.

'Yes, I do,' he replied in a low voice, looking down at the table, avoiding her stare.

'No, you don't,' she shouted. 'She is a siren, a witch who knows nothing but to seduce men and turn them mad. Please do not let Sahay use you to get a spicy story. I cannot let you do it, Avik. You must know what happened to the journalists who went to her. I don't want you to share the same fate. Please,' Trisha was almost begging him.

He saw on her face the fear of losing him forever.

'I will be fine, trust me. This is important to me,' Avik tried to reassure her.

But was he sure himself? He had no answer.

He dropped her home and as a goodbye, hugged her tightly, thinking it might be the last time he held her in his arms. She clutched his shirt, not wanting to let go.

He expected her to ask him to come up to her beautiful apartment so they could make it a night to remember. But she did not. She would not do him any such favour, now that he had chosen the assignment over her. She gave him a peck on his cheek and ran into the building.

On the entire ride back home, he kept wondering if Trisha was right.

Avik got home with a heavy heart. Something was making him uneasy, but it was not their break-up. Trisha's words had made him nervous.

Is Sahay just using me, as Trisha believes? What happened to the journalists who worked on the story? Avik was full of doubts as he packed for his trip to Delhi.

He needed answers before he set forth himself. He made a cup of tea and sat down to google Kalki Rajput. Stories about her accidental death or suicide or murder came up. He read some of the headlines.

Millionare Wife Kalki Rajput Drowns Herself

Wife Commits Suicide, Daughter Goes Insane

In Death Did They Part: Ronit Rajput Loses Wife to the Yamuna

He clicked on a story about Ananki's madness.

He read the entire article. Then he read several more. None of the articles provided any details about the reasons behind Ananki's sudden insanity except her mother's death.

Can anyone love their mother so much that her death would make them insane? he wondered.

It was strange to him. He looked at the clock. It was 2.50 a.m. Not a very good time to call Sahay, but he had no choice. The sleepy voice on the other end seemed quite reluctant to answer.

'I want to know the names of the journalists who have worked on Ananki's story earlier,' he asked Sahay, coming straight to the point.

'I don't know their names, but I have heard that they were reduced to such a terrible plight after they started working on her case that they couldn't cover the entire story,' Sahay sleepily replied.

'What plight?'

'One of them met with an accident and died on the spot. Nothing regarding Ananki's version of her mother's death was found in his belongings. Another one went missing and hasn't been found till date. The third one was thought to be missing too, but after a year it was discovered that he had been admitted into a mental institution. It is said that he had been doing drugs for a long time. Anything else you want to ask?'

'No. Nothing.'

'Are you sure you want to go to Delhi or have you changed your mind?' Sahay asked almost tauntingly.

'No. I am going to leave for Delhi tomorrow,' Avik replied and hung up.

The ceiling above his head seemed to be spinning. The day had proved to be a very difficult one. He fell on his bed; he had to discover what no else had been able to.

This assignment is not just access to a story but the fulfilment of a dream. I have waited long enough for a break like this; I cannot wait any longer. Nothing in this world can stop me; neither love nor fear can pull me back. I am ready. Avik covered himself with a sheet, falling asleep almost immediately.

2

The positive thoughts he had had before falling asleep made Avik wake up feeling far more optimistic. The first thing he did was to clean his flat. When he was done, he looked around fondly. This was his home and he wanted to come back to it after the assignment was over. He went to every corner of his flat, caressing small objects that he never otherwise paid any attention to, objects that safeguarded the memories he had made in this city.

Avik stopped in front of the photo that adorned his living-room wall. It had been taken at Trisha's birthday a year ago. She had her arms around his neck as he put cake on her tiny nose. Her pearly white teeth gleamed in a smile that reflected the happiness in her heart. He reached out to touch Trisha's face. His moist eyes betrayed how terribly he was going to miss her. But he had made his choice.

He reached the airport early in the hope that Trisha would come to see him off. He called her twice but she did not answer her phone. After leaving many messages he finally got a reply from her. She could not come to meet him.

Of course her presentation is more important. How can I blame her? She loves what she does; so do I. Our love for our respective dreams is greater than the love we have for each other.

Although parting from Trisha was difficult, Avik knew that he had no choice. It would be better if he directed his thoughts to the task ahead of him. To Ananki.

He boarded the flight, switched off his mobile phone and closed his eyes so the darkness could envelop him. He had loved the dark ever since he was a little boy. It was the source of his imagination. Strangely, it was the one thing he trusted the most, for it revealed what was missed by the logical eye. He let himself float freely in its grey realm. He wanted the darkness to show him Ananki before he actually saw her. He whispered her name thrice and saw her standing right in front of him as if her spirit had been conjured. She walked towards him and sat in the vacant seat adjacent to his. Was he prepared to look at her? She leaned towards his left ear as if to say something. He was anxious to hear the first words from her.

'So, you are adamant on committing suicide. Mind you, you will regret this decision,' he heard her say.

Wait a minute, this is a very familiar voice. He turned to her. It was Trisha, shouting at him. Strangely, he could not hear a single word. He got up, went to the emergency exit, opened it and jumped out of the aircraft. How he had longed for this fresh air! It was chilling and his body was going numb.

He spread his arms. It was exhilarating. He wished he could stop the passage of time. He loosened his watch and let it fall, hoping he could escape time, but it would not stop for him even if he let it go. He knew nothing more except being in free fall. He looked down. He felt he was looking at a Google Earth map.

'Excuse me, sir, sorry to wake you up, but we have landed at Delhi airport,' the airhostess said, tapping his shoulder.

He woke up. Nearly the entire aircraft had emptied out. He moved towards the exit with a heavy head.

Avik took a taxi to the flat Sahay had arranged. It was a studio apartment, barely big enough for him. He relaxed on the couch and closed his eyes. An image of a being, half-serpent, half-woman, flashed before his eyes. He quickly opened them, sat up, reached for his phone and the next thing he knew, his mother's voice was on the other end.

'Avik, are you okay? What happened? Why are you not saying anything? Can you hear me, Avik?'

'Yes, Ma. I am in Delhi,' he replied, not knowing what else to say.

He could not understand why he had dialled his mother's number. They had not spoken to each other in months, since he had made her meet Trisha. She had thought Trisha was too independent to be his wife and would not settle down with him, at least not for the next several years.

According to his mother, it was high time he got married. The thirties were the age for rearing children, not for wandering about as a bachelor. Avik, on the other hand, wanted to make it big before taking on marital responsibilities. This was his last chance and he was determined to accomplish something.

'Where are you staying? Why don't you stay at home?' she asked.

'I am here on an important assignment, Ma. I can't stay at home,' Avik replied.

'You think I will disturb you?' she asked in the tone that Avik had always disliked. It was neither a taunt nor a question, but a sad truth that filled him with guilt.

'It is not like that, Ma, but I don't want to bother you. If I stay there, I know you won't sleep until I do and I won't be able to work like that. Please understand,' Avik pleaded.

'Are you still upset with me because of the things I said about Trisha? That was my opinion, but you know I will respect your decision,' she said.

'I know, Ma. Goodnight.'

'Avik, I won't interfere with your plans. I just want to be sure that you are fine. You don't sound okay to me,' she insisted.

'Ma, I'm fine. I am tired because of the journey. I will visit you soon. Take care,' Avik said and hung up.

It was foolish of me to have told Ma that I am in Delhi. Moreover, the fact that he had not been able to tell his mother that he had broken up with Trisha disturbed him. *It would have comforted her. She has tried her best to hide it, but I know that Trisha is not someone she wants to share me with.*

The two women made him feel like a failure as a son and a boyfriend. He hoped the next woman in his life would bring him the long-awaited success. He started thinking about this woman as he lay back on the couch and gazed up at the ceiling with a blank expression. Suddenly, something struck him.

I can search the Internet for a picture of Ananki Rajput, he thought as he rushed to fetch his laptop bag.

He typed her name in the search bar and pressed enter. Of the several hundred images that popped up, the one that caught his attention first was one of the Parthenon in Athens. He clicked on it and discovered that 'Ananki' was derived from the name of the Greek goddess 'Ananke', who was one of the Greek primordial deities. She marked the beginning of the cosmos along with her husband Chronos. Ananke was the goddess of inevitability and fate.

That is indeed a strange name, strange yet inevitable, he thought.

But all he cared about at the moment was what Ananki Rajput looked like. He searched for images of her. There she was. He breathed a sigh of relief on seeing a young girl with long hair, a wheatish complexion, sharp nose and big eyes. He could not be sure if her eyes were dark brown or black, but something told him that they were dark brown, the colour of the dark chocolate brownie he had always loved.

He looked at another picture, a full-length shot. She appeared to be quite tall for an Indian woman, at least 5' 8". She had a slender waist and a charming smile. The beautiful smile made him smile too. She had a girl-next-door look.

Avik realized that he was very tired. He needed a sound sleep. A sleep untarnished by dreams. *Lucky are the people who can forget their dreams. Why do I remember them? Why do they occupy such a huge space in my mind? Remembrance can be a painful experience. It brings lament for the moments that are lost in time, the moments that died and are buried in the past, the moments that can never be resurrected. Memories float like ghosts in the subconscious, making appearances through dreams, troubling to the point of torture, making the conscious mind beg for some solace,* he deliberated as he went to fetch a bottle of whisky from his bag. He needed something that would soothe his mind, keep the thoughts and memories at bay. What better than a few large pegs of whisky? He drank till he dropped off.

The following morning, Avik took his first good look at the studio apartment. He did not like it at all. It was too small even for one person. There was little room for him to pace up and down when he needed to think. There was no writing table. This vexed him the most. He hated the sight of the ugly couch and the little table it was paired with.

The bathroom was worse. There was little room for him to scrub his back and he bruised his elbow while bathing.

When he finally left, he realized that there were no general stores within a two-kilometre radius of the flat. He could not find an autorickshaw either. He was hungry, his elbow throbbed and he had to walk to find any sign of civilization. It was not a very good start to his 'mission Ananki'. He was annoyed and cursed Sahay.

That son of a bitch must be having his breakfast in his air-conditioned cabin while here I am, wandering around with an empty stomach in the Delhi heat. He treats me as if I am nothing more than a street dog that gets whipped for barking unnecessarily.

Finally, after a long walk, Avik saw an autorickshaw coming towards him. He stopped it and jumped inside, instructing the driver to take him to Connaught Place.

'Why haven't you turned on the meter?' Avik inquired after a few minutes.

'It doesn't work,' the driver replied casually.

'Then how much will you charge?' Avik was getting increasingly agitated.

'Two hundred rupees.'

Avik wanted to smack the driver for even suggesting such an exorbitant fare.

Nothing was working out as he had planned. He had come to Delhi to make it big, but all he was doing was wandering hungry on its scorching streets with a bruised elbow.

After battling his hunger and thirst for two hours he finally reached his favourite food and beer joint in Connaught Place.

He ordered a plate of chicken tikka and a pitcher of beer.

The heat had gotten to him. He needed to cool down. The beer helped.

He was almost done with his meal when he saw a girl approaching his table. As she drew close, he recognized her. She was Khyati, a friend of his from school in Aligarh. They had also travelled on the same University Special bus to college.

'Look at you! You look so different,' Avik exclaimed even before she had reached his table.

He could not believe his eyes. Khyati had always been a tomboy. Seeing her in a kurti and long skirt amazed him.

Her fair, glowing skin, a little eyeliner, mauve lipstick and big silver earrings she was wearing all combined to make her look beautiful.

'Different in a good way or bad way?' she asked, giving him a hug.

'Good,' he said, smiling. 'It's been so long. How have you been?' Avik asked as he hugged her, noticing that she had become more voluptuous.

'Been great, and you?'

'Sit, sit. There's so much to catch up on,' Avik gestured to the chair next to him.

'I'm here with my friends,' she replied politely, pointing to a table in the corner of the restaurant, her glass bangles tinkling.

'Ah, I see! Your girl gang, eh! Why don't you tell them you have better company now?' Avik chuckled.

'Is that not for me to decide?' Khyati played along.

'But to decide you must experience my company as well,' Avik replied.

He desperately wanted her to stay with him and turn what remained of the day into a good one.

Khyati smiled. 'All right, I'll just go and tell my friends that I won't be joining them.'

When she returned, she sat next to him on the couch.

'You have not changed at all. The same happy-go-lucky attitude, the same always-smiling face, the same always-part-of-a-girl-gang. You know, back in school everyone thought you were a lesbian. I just hope that it isn't true.' Avik smiled as he whispered the last part.

'Oh my God, really? And all this while I wondered why no one ever sent me gifts on Valentine's Day, wrapped up in shimmering paper, delivered with the aid of a common friend.' Khyati laughed, winking at Avik, reminding him of the time when he had once made her the mediator for sending a gift to his first crush at school.

'Maybe someone did, but your girlfriend who was supposed to pass it on stole it away from you,' Avik teased.

'Oh no! I swear to hereby forsake all my girlfriends. From now on I will only enjoy the company of my boy friends,' she laughed.

'How many boyfriends do you have?' Avik asked, trying to flirt with her.

'See, there's the catch. I said "boy friends" not "boyfriends", who are very few, I must add,' she said and giggled as she turned to the waiter to give the order for both of them.

She remembers what I like, Avik thought as Khyati ordered his favourite dish and a pitcher of beer.

As they shared the fried pomfret, Avik learnt that Khyati was doing her PhD in psychology. He saved her contact number, knowing he might need it soon. When he told her that he would be covering a story on someone with a mental illness, Khyati said that she would be more than willing to help him out.

When they left together, they realized that it was evening already. She rushed to take the metro to Dwarka while he had other plans.

There was something about Connaught Place that fascinated him. The countless white pillars of the shopping arcades stood erect in eternal glory. The green lawns of the Central Park added to the beauty. The cool spray from the fountains was refreshing. *Delhi indeed has a charm no other place in India has*, he thought as he sat in the park.

He stayed there for a while, looking at young couples arm in arm, kids playing football on the grassy slope and hundreds of pigeons fluttering through the air. It filled him with peace and positivity.

It was late when he got up to leave. The thought of going back to the dungeon that was his studio apartment vexed him. He called Sahay and insisted that he move him to another apartment. To put him off, Sahay asked Avik to stay in the flat till he could find something better. However, Avik didn't fall for the trick and said that he would move to a hotel till a better apartment could be arranged. Sahay had no choice but to agree. He wanted this story at any cost.

Avik was pleased. This was perhaps the first time that Sahay had agreed to any of his demands. It seemed that the Ananki Rajput story was as important for Sahay as it was for him.

Sahay's dependence on him gave Avik a strange sense of achievement. For the first time he realized his own importance.

The success of this assignment depends solely on me. I can't fail this time.

On the way back to the flat, Avik speculated about the possible reasons for Ananki's madness.

He felt a shiver of anticipation at the thought of meeting her.

How will the meeting go? Will I be able to break the ice between her and the world? Or will her story remain locked in her mind? he wondered as he gazed at the purple-red sky.

He had no answers to any of these questions. He knew he would have to wait till they unfolded. Right now, all he could hope for was a positive outcome.

Avik checked into a hotel of his choice. Sahay seemed upset that Avik was staying in a hotel on the company's expense despite having his own house in Delhi. Avik, however, made it clear to Sahay that it would not be possible for him to work on the assignment from his own home, given the inquisitive nature of his mother. Most of the times, Avik didn't quite like the questions his mother had in store for him whenever he went to stay with her, especially related to his relationship and marriage. He was sure that this time would be no different. It was better to have a different accommodation.

Avik's father had passed away ten years ago and as his mother was on her own, he could not bear to see her suffer for any reason.

Shakuntala was a graceful woman. Once a teacher in Aligarh, she took voluntary retirement after her husband's death to move to his house in Delhi, as per his last wish. The move was welcomed by Avik as he was fed up of being bullied by his cousins, with whom they had lived in Aligarh.

Avik thought that Shakuntala was the perfect Indian woman. Her crisp cotton saree, her long hair neatly tied in a bun, her big red kumkum bindi, which she did not wear after her husband's demise, her soft voice, her love for making her home look beautiful, her excellent cooking, her fine taste in music, all of this made her the ideal.

Avik knew it was hard to find all these qualities in one woman. He had always believed his father to be a very lucky man. He particularly admired his mother for bringing him up almost single-handedly. It pained him to think that in return, he was not able to take care of her as he should. The only thing he did for her was to send her half of his salary every month so she could live a comfortable life in Delhi, even though it meant that he was left with little to indulge in luxuries. He had just enough to buy books and spend on a good time with friends every now and then.

Avik decided that he would pay his mother a surprise visit for dinner. On the way, he felt a strong urge to see her happy. It was a strange urge, as if after tonight he would not remain the same, as if tomorrow would change everything. He stopped at a flower shop.

'They are for my mother. She has always loved them more than roses,' he smiled as he told the florist to make a bouquet of twenty-one purple carnations.

Shakuntala welcomed him with open arms and glistening eyes. He had never seen her cry, except on the day he lost his father. He had always felt that her dewy eyes kept within them some secret that she never shared with him. Something he dared not ask her.

'How do you always manage to prepare dinner so quickly, Ma?' Avik asked as he sat at the table, waiting for his mother to serve him.

'I have a magic wand with me. You know what it is called?' Shakuntala had been asking Avik this ever since he was a little boy.

Just like always, he pretended he did not know the answer.

'The magic wand is called love,' she said and smiled as she served him his dinner.

Avik could tell that his mother was happy, which made him happy too. He was glad that she did not ask him about his work in Delhi. He did not like lying to her and he could not tell her the truth. So it was best not talked about.

She showed him a vase she had recently painted. It was a beautifully done piece of artwork. He smiled fondly at her and went back to the couch, not knowing when he fell asleep.

It was his mother's chanting in the morning that woke him up. He felt refreshed and much better than he had the previous day. She had prepared his favourite aloo paranthas for breakfast.

Will I ever find a woman who understands me as well as Ma? Someone whom I don't have to tell things, someone with whom I can share a silent channel of communication, just like the one I have with Ma, Avik wondered as he listened to her chanting in her sweet voice.

She finally asked him at the breakfast table, 'Is everything fine?'

He knew she had sensed that something was wrong. Despite knowing that it would not satisfy her, all he could do was nod his head in affirmation.

He stood up to leave and touched her feet. She planted a kiss on his forehead. He hugged her, not knowing when he would be able to meet her again. It felt like a final farewell to him.

'Goodbye, Ma,' he said with a heavy heart and walked out.

Avik went to meet Khyati that afternoon at her flat in Vijay Nagar. Her father had helped her with the down payment for it, but she managed the EMIs by spending wisely and renting out the two spare rooms to paying guests. The flat had beautiful interiors and reflected Khyati's love for ethnic décor.

Avik learnt that apart from doing research for her PhD, Khyati was assisting a psychiatrist, Dr Tarun Bhalla, on a part-time basis. She was the epitome of the modern Indian woman: strong-willed, independent and with the zest to succeed on her own terms. She was single and not ready to mingle unless her mind clicked with the man.

As Avik sat talking to her, Khyati perceived a certain anxiousness about him. She could not help but ask the reason for it. Avik knew there was no one else with whom he could share his concerns. She could help him with this case. He told her that he had not been able to make much progress as far as Ananki Rajput was concerned.

Khyati had only one thing to say, 'Get hold of her psychiatrist first.'

She was right. It was important for him to get acquainted with Ananki's case history before he met her.

'I can help you with this case. Any kind of aberration in the working of the human mind fascinates me. I would love to study her case,' Khyati readily volunteered to assist him.

'Okay, then let's visit Ananki's psychiatrist together. It is indeed quite depressing to be alone in Delhi. Your support will give me some much-needed confidence,' Avik said, placing his hand on hers.

As soon as Avik got back to his hotel room, he pulled out the list of important contacts Sahay had given him. He saw that Dr Vijay Kaul had been looking after Ananki's case since November 2006, soon after Kalki Rajput's accident and death. He had a private clinic in Greater Kailash. Avik called the clinic and fixed an appointment with him as a patient. He was not sure whether he would be entertained if he told the truth and he could not afford failure right at the start.

That night as he lay in his bed, he felt a sense of comfort at having finally taken the first step towards his goal and at the thought that he was not alone.

3

The appointment with Dr Vijay Kaul was at 11.00 a.m. Avik met Khyati an hour earlier so they could discuss how to broach the subject of Ananki with the doctor.

'We should tell Dr Kaul the reason for this meeting right at the beginning,' Khyati suggested as they headed to the clinic in an autorickshaw.

'No, if we tell him, he might not entertain us at all.' Avik shook his head as he scribbled down the questions he wanted to ask Dr Kaul.

'I had a word with Dr Tarun this morning and he advised me not to keep Dr Kaul in the dark even for a moment. With his experience, he'll know immediately that you are feigning an illness. The last thing you want to do is raise his ire,' Khyati warned Avik.

He said nothing, as they had arrived at the clinic. Dr Kaul's assistant asked them to wait in the reception area. They were early and the wait was difficult for Avik. Every passing minute increased his nervousness. Khyati nudged him, a sign for him to relax. He tried to divert his mind by focusing on the room.

Three huge bronze-coloured couches took up half the space. Amidst them was a round glass table piled high with health magazines. The reception desk was placed in one corner. In the opposite corner, a water cooler and coffee machine rested on a marble counter. A huge poster depicting the human brain caught his eye. Initially, the poster disturbed him, but the more he studied it, the more engrossed he became in it. *How can such a small space hold such an infinitely vast amount of knowledge, imagination, memories and dreams,* he wondered, staring at the poster.

His eye was next caught by a black-and-white photograph in a golden frame on the wall in front of him. Avik pointed to it to ask Khyati if she knew who the man in the photograph was.

'That's Dr Alfred Adler, founder of the school of individual psychology.'

As she was telling Avik more about the doctor's work, a male voice interrupted her.

'He was the first major figure to break away from Freud's psychoanalysis to form an independent school of psychotherapy and personality theory. Hello, I am Dr Vijay Kaul and you seemed to be quite interested in psychology, else you would not have known Dr Adler.'

Khyati smiled and told the doctor briefly about her field of study, which broke the ice.

Dr Kaul was a short, bald man in a grey suit. His belly made him appear rounder than he was. He wore round spectacles with a golden frame and the matching chain that hung from them was looped around his neck. Avik was distracted by his ears, which he thought were too large for the doctor's face.

Dr Kaul invited them both into the consultation room. He seemed to be interested in what Khyati had to say, for in most cases only the patient was allowed in to see the doctor.

'Please be seated, Avik,' the doctor said, shifting his attention from Khyati to him. 'How can I help you?'

Avik exchanged a quick glance with Khyati. She nodded slightly in affirmation. He took a deep breath and decided that it was the right time to tell Dr Kaul the motive behind this meeting.

'I have come to you with an objective and not an ailment, and only you can help me,' Avik said and paused to see the doctor's reaction.

Dr Kaul was surprised. He removed his glasses, opened the file lying in front of him and skimmed through the patient form Avik had filled in, giving him a piercing stare when he was done.

'So you are a journalist. If you wanted an interview, you could have told me as much. There was no need to turn up as a patient. Or did you want to see for yourself how capable or incapable I was?' Dr Kaul smiled scornfully as he said those last words.

Avik sat quietly, not knowing what to say. Nervousness made him clutch the arms of the chair tightly. He thought it would be better to come to the point right away.

'It is Ananki Rajput's case that has brought me to you,' he said in a low voice.

Dr Kaul started. He looked upset.

'How dare you?' he demanded angrily, before stopping himself in an effort to regain his composure. He took a deep breath and continued, 'I am sorry to disappoint you, but I will not be able to help you regarding this matter. You may leave now.'

Khyati stood up, but Avik remained seated. He could not leave without learning at least a few facts about Ananki.

'Look, Dr Kaul, this case is really important to me,' Avik pleaded.

'How does that matter to me? I cannot break the rules just because something is important to you. Now if you will please leave me alone. Thanks,' Dr Kaul replied, pointing towards the door.

'I have put everything at stake for this case. Getting to know Ananki is my only hope for uncovering what actually happened. You are a very successful man. You may not understand the sacrifices I have had to make so I could come to Delhi to try and solve this mystery. It's crucial to my career,' Avik beseeched the doctor.

Khyati looked from one to the other and placed a hand on Avik's shoulder, a sign for him to get up.

'That does not give you the right to put another person's career at stake,' Dr Kaul responded angrily.

'Dr Kaul, I would never reveal that you were my source. Not even to my boss.'

Khyati squeezed Avik's shoulder in an attempt to make him get up, but he remained immobile.

Dr Kaul turned his choler on Khyati. 'I would have expected more sense from you, young lady. Being knowledgeable about this profession, how could you think you would be able to extract a patient's history from me? Surely you know confidentiality is one of the basic rules of psychiatric practice. Tell this gentleman to leave at once, else I will have to ask security to throw him out.'

Having said that, Dr Kaul got up and strode out of the room.

Khyati quickly followed him. But Avik remained in his seat. He felt he had been checkmated at the very first move.

He felt like a failure. His hope of proving his worth had left the room while he was left sitting there, clasping the arms of the chair he was seated on. He was on the verge of a meltdown when Dr Kaul's assistant came in to tell him that Khyati was waiting for him outside the clinic.

He picked himself up and left without looking at the assistant. He walked past Khyati who looked worried, but he made no effort to speak to her. She followed him, trying to keep pace with him. The more she tried, the faster he walked. He did not want her to be a witness to his pathetic self. They walked for about half an hour, one behind the other. Then Khyati stopped and called his name, panting for breath. Avik looked back; she was trailing him by almost a hundred metres. He ran back to her, took out a bottle of water from his bag and made her drink.

'I am so sorry, Khyati. I was just so upset.' Avik was full of remorse.

'It's okay. Let's get an autorickshaw. I can't walk anymore.'

They returned to his hotel in silence. She ordered room service and Avik got himself a beer from the mini fridge.

The meeting had exhausted both of them. It was dusk, but Avik had not spoken a single word since they had sat in the autorickshaw.

His silence worried her.

'Can I stay here for a while?' Khyati asked him, not wanting to leave him alone in this state.

He nodded. Relieved, she smiled at him. 'Okay, now enough of this tragedy king avatar. Let's watch a movie,' she suggested, unzipping his laptop bag and taking out his laptop and hard disk.

Avik was surprised by how much she had changed since she had first moved to Delhi. She had been a simple girl from Aligarh. Sheltered by her conservative family, she had hardly spoken to anyone.

Delhi has done her good, he thought.

Khyati suddenly asked him about Trisha. 'Is Trisha planning to visit Delhi too?'

He smiled at her as she selected his favourite Bollywood movie, the classic *Pyaasa*.

'Delhi is not on Trisha's priority list,' he replied, his eyes fixed on the laptop screen.

Khyati was watching him closely. She had liked him ever since they had been in school together. When she had moved to Delhi for college, she had had no friends or contacts in the city. Except for Avik. They had become good friends after they had cleared their senior secondary exams.

Avik had pursued a degree in journalism while she had studied psychology. Every day they would take the same University Special bus to North Campus and chat all the way.

Bunking lectures to go watch movies, roaming the streets of 'K-Nags' – they did it all together. She was the one girl he felt comfortable with and she was aware of it. No matter how much she liked him, the last thing she had wanted was to upset their equation.

Khyati wanted to lighten Avik's mood.

'Do you remember the time when you forced me to come to one of your "eat, drink and be merry" parties?' she asked, waggling her eyebrows and smiling.

'The ones where smoking only cigarettes and drinking only soda was considered a sin,' he chuckled as he took a sip of beer.

'Yeah, those "out-of-the-world" parties of yours.'

'Remember when we coaxed you to smoke and I gave you a step-by-step demonstration on how to successfully inhale on your first attempt?' Avik asked her.

'Of course I remember. I choked on the very first puff and couldn't stop coughing. I was so humiliated! You rushed and brought water for me.'

'Immediately after which you insisted on a second try. No matter how much I tried to stop you, you were adamant on showing us that you could do it too. And you did. How time flies!' Avik put his hand on her shoulder and squeezed it gently.

Khyati felt butterflies in her stomach at his touch. Disconcerted, she tried to distract herself.

'Do you have a smoke?' she asked him.

He was startled.

'You smoke?'

'Well, I have been practising for the last six years,' she replied.

They had a hearty laugh, a much-needed one after what had happened in the afternoon.

Avik lit a cigarette and handed it to her.

She took it, paused the movie and then shut down the laptop.

'I thought someone had stayed over to watch a movie,' Avik said and gulped down the rest of the beer in the bottle.

'I am sure you must have watched it over a thousand times.' She took the bottle from him, went to the refrigerator and pulled out another. She went to the table and filled both the mugs lying on it, handing one to him.

Then she grabbed him by his wrist and pulled him out of the room. He soon found himself on the terrace of the hotel.

The hotel building was much higher than the ones adjacent to it, giving them an amazing view of the lights of Paharganj, the hub for cheap hotels in Delhi. They gazed down at the sight for a while, forgetting everything else. The colourful neon lights looked like something out of fantasyland.

'Look at those lights. Let's divide them into two kinds, blinking and non-blinking. Which kind do you find yourself more connected to?' Avik asked.

Khyati gazed at the lights for a while, as if reading silent signals that they were sending her.

'The non-blinking ones tell me to stand firm through the worst of times,' she replied.

Avik smiled at her reply and turned his gaze to the street to look at the lights once more.

'I feel a close connection to the blinking ones. Are they not just like our lives? One moment they are bright and shiny, ready to face any challenge that the darkness has in store for them; the next moment they become one with the darkness, as if submitting themselves to its might. We humans remain content when times are good, but in times of turmoil we become gloomy and desperate,' Avik ended with a sigh.

'I agree, but that is why I prefer the non-blinking lights, as they inspire us to stay cheerful and bright amidst the darkest of times,' Khyati replied.

'Don't you think you're being too idealistic? I mean, when times are against you, it's normal for you to be gloomy. One can only hope to be happy in such times, but in reality the shadow of stress always hovers over one's mind,' Avik said, looking straight into her eyes.

'Well, it is Delhi that is behind my idealistic positivism.' Khyati laughed.

She held up her beer mug in a toast.

'To Delhi,' she said.

He laughed, not knowing whether she was high on the beer or Delhi.

'Bottoms up then,' he said as he raised his mug, clanked it against hers and drank till the last drop.

They looked at each other and cracked up. Neither knew why they were laughing, but soon they were sitting on the terrace floor in splits. All of a sudden everything went quiet as they finally stopped to catch their breath. Avik stretched out next to Khyati.

He had missed lying on a terrace and admiring the stars. The race to survive and succeed in a competitive world had snatched away these little pleasures of life. He felt content, not just in watching the stars but watching the stars with her.

'I have wanted to do this for a very long time,' he said, turning to look at her.

'Do what? Get drunk?' she asked.

'No. Lie in the silence of the dark and gaze at the skies. It's heavenly,' Avik exclaimed as he looked at the full moon above him. All his life he had felt a deep connection with the moon, especially when it was full.

'Don't tell me you and Trisha never did this together?' Khyati was surprised.

'We did not have time for such "stupid stuff"', he replied.

'Who says it's stupid? I feel it is one of the best ways to release all the negativity and stress that one has collected during the day so that one can sleep well at night. There is no point in sleeping for seven to eight hours if all you have inside is junk,' she said, smiling up at the stars.

They both went silent for a while.

He did not know when he passed out. The chirping of birds and the noise of the horns from the street woke him up the next morning. He turned around to look for Khyati. She wasn't there. He went back to his room and found her engrossed in the newspaper. He thought it better not to disturb her and left to get them tea.

On his way, Avik thought about how he could extract information from Dr Kaul's office. He called the doctor's assistant and offered him ten thousand rupees in return for any information he could provide about Ananki. The assistant told Avik to transfer the money to his account first.

Avik had to take the risk. He stopped by the Internet café adjacent to his hotel and transferred the sum to the assistant's account. The assistant in return scanned and emailed him the most recent letter in Ananki's file. It was one of the most expensive pieces of information Avik had ever collected.

When he got back to the hotel room, Khyati was still reading the newspaper. He handed her a cup of tea and kept the printout of the letter on the coffee table.

'What is the breaking news today?' he inquired, heading to the bathroom.

'Your favourite thirty-seven-year-old actress is pregnant,' she read aloud.

He guffawed as he came out. 'That's not news. That's a miracle.'

Both of them burst out laughing and Khyati accidentally spilt some tea on the printout Avik had kept on the table. Avik rushed to clean it up. Khyati sensed that it was something important and picked it up. It was a note, written on Dr Vijay Kaul's letterhead, referring Ananki to a Dr Neerja Sharma. It included the address of Dr Sharma's NGO, which looked after patients with mental ailments who were unable to get treatment from competent doctors and reputed hospitals.

'How did you get this?' Khyati asked, surprised.

'Don't forget I'm a journalist. We are good at getting things that we want,' he replied, grinning.

Avik took the printout from her and looked at the address. The NGO was in Chanakyapuri. He wanted to meet Dr Neerja and through her, hopefully Ananki, but before that he had to meet someone else.

He asked Khyati to get ready quickly and meet him at the hotel entrance. Then he ran downstairs to look for an autorickshaw.

As they sat in the rickshaw, Avik told the driver to take them to Greater Kailash.

'Why are we heading to Dr Kaul's and not to Dr Sharma's NGO?' Khyati looked confused.

'Dr Kaul has referred Ananki to another doctor, which means that she is no longer his patient. No rules apply now. He will have to tell us everything he knows about the case,' Avik said.

'What if he still refuses?' Khyati asked.

'He won't. You just watch.'

Avik was brimming with confidence.

When they met Dr Kaul, Avik confronted him with what he had found out.

'When Ananki Rajput was reported missing, you knew where she was. How could you keep such an important piece of information to yourself? You should have told the police her whereabouts. You could be charged under the Indian Penal Code for what you did,' Avik challenged the doctor.

'I didn't know she was missing,' Dr Kaul replied casually.

'The news of the millionaire's daughter going missing spread through the city like a forest fire, it was telecast by every single news channel, the print media posted full-page advertisements with her photograph, the police requested citizens to help them in their search, so don't try and make me believe, Dr Kaul, that you didn't know she was missing,' Avik said, placing both his hands on the table and leaning towards Dr Kaul, staring him directly in the eye.

'But I didn't know her whereabouts. Mr Rajput just stopped her visits, how would I know where she was?' Dr Kaul insisted, trying to avoid Avik's stare.

'Of course you did. It was you who advised Mr Rajput to shift her to Dr Neerja's NGO. I have proof with me and can present it to the police if you don't help me.'

Dr Kaul felt exposed. Nonetheless, he refused when Avik asked him for a copy of Ananki's case file.

'I cannot give you a patient's file. It is against the rules,' Dr Kaul muttered nervously, wiping the sweat dripping from his large, shining forehead.

'A copy of the file, please, or I will have to call the police.' Avik reached for the telephone on the table.

Dr Kaul had no option but to agree. He called in his assistant and told him to make a copy of Ananki Rajput's case file.

'Copy every single page,' Avik added.

It took the assistant almost half an hour to return with the copy of the file. Avik flipped through the pages and then turned to Dr Kaul.

'I have one last question for you. Although I know the answer, I want you to confirm it. Who wanted Ananki to disappear?'

'Mr Rajput. He paid me a huge amount for keeping the whereabouts to myself,' Dr Kaul replied.

'Thank you,' Avik said as he closed the file and left, followed by Khyati.

The moment they were out of the clinic, Khyati started yelling at him.

'Are you completely out of your mind? He could file an FIR against us for this. I can't believe what you just did, Avik. We could land in serious trouble.'

Her eyes were red, brimming with anger.

'Nothing will happen to us, for Dr Kaul is guilty himself. He needs to protect himself rather than complain against us,' Avik reassured her.

'But you cannot just hurl such serious accusations at someone, Avik. You need to be more careful,' Khyati advised him.

'I knew what I was doing, Khyati. I have the proof with me. The whole world thought Ananki was under Dr Kaul's care when she went missing. Later, her father said that she had been admitted to an asylum because she was mentally ill, but he also said that she was still being treated by Dr Kaul,' Avik replied.

Khyati knew there was no point in arguing with him since the deed had already been done.

'The good thing that came out of it is the file,' Avik said as he handed it to her.

Khyati opened it to read the case history. She saw that Ananki had been diagnosed with depression.

'Dr Kaul initially treated her with fluoxetine hydrochloride, an antidepressant,' she said as she quickly turned to the prescription on the last page. 'He also prescribed chlorpromazine. I don't know much about this medicine except for the fact that it causes a strong dulling of the mind. I know who would know more. Let's go meet Dr Bhalla,' she suggested, closing the file.

'Is he like Dr Kaul? If he is, it would be better if you dealt with him,' Avik asked her on the way.

'Don't worry. Dr Bhalla is a warm-hearted individual who believes in addressing a patient's actual problems rather than attempting to control their behaviour through psychotropic drugs. According to him, such medications can often make a patient's condition worse. His method is mild but very effective. Talk therapy can work miracles that most drugs cannot. But it requires a lot of patience and time, which is in short supply for most psychiatrists nowadays,' Khyati explained.

Dr Tarun Bhalla was in his study. He was sitting in an armchair, reading, when the servant showed Khyati and Avik into the room. On seeing them, he got up to greet his visitors. He was a handsome man but had a clumsy gait, Avik noticed as the doctor walked towards them.

After introducing Avik, Khyati came straight to the point. 'How serious is the condition of a patient who has been prescribed chlorpromazine?' she asked.

Dr Tarun was taken aback for a second. He cleared his throat to speak. 'Chlorpromazine is a neuroleptic drug, which means that it can cause a serious dulling of the mind. It can result in a kind of chemical lobotomy, which is to say that it can seriously compromise the functioning of the frontal lobes.'

'What is the function of the frontal lobes?' Avik asked, looking a little perplexed.

'The frontal lobes are unique to human beings and are the seat of the higher functions such as love, empathy, insight, creativity, rationality, judgement and so on. Without the frontal lobes it is impossible to be "human" in the fullest sense of the word,' Dr Tarun explained.

Before he could continue, he was interrupted by a female voice.

'To cut a long story short, chlorpromazine can seriously impair a person's sense of self and their environment,' a lady said as she walked into the study carrying a tea tray.

She smiled at them as she kept the tea tray on the table.

'Meet my wife, Dr Neerja. Or I should have said meet Dr Neerja, my wife, since she is a doctor first, then my wife. I think she is fonder of her patients than she is of me,' Dr Tarun said, and he and his wife both laughed.

Avik glanced at Khyati. *Is she thinking of the same possibility that I am?* he wondered.

To confirm his suspicion, he handed Dr Neerja Ananki's case file. For a while she just gazed at it, lost in thought. The name seemed familiar to her, since she did not open the file at once.

'I am surprised that someone still cares to find out about Ananki. In the last two years, not a single person has inquired about her, including her own father,' Dr Neerja finally said, handing Avik a cup of tea.

So she is none other than the Dr Neerja Sharma to whom Dr Kaul had referred Ananki. It is she who treated Ananki after one of the best psychiatrists in India abandoned her. Was it her large-heartedness or did she take the case up as a challenge? Avik pondered as he sipped his tea.

After they had finished their tea, too many questions whirled in Avik's mind. But before asking them, he wanted to put together the scattered pieces of the jigsaw puzzle that was this case, in order to get a better understanding of the information they had collected.

As they got up to leave, Dr Neerja asked if she could keep the case file to study Ananki's medication history. Avik agreed.

'Will you help me meet her?' was the only question he could manage to ask Dr Neerja.

She looked at him for a moment as if to guess his thoughts, then replied with a faint smile, 'I will, provided she wants to meet you. See you later.'

Avik nodded and they left. He did not want to go back to his hotel room. Moreover, looking for autorickshaws in the heat was getting on his nerves. He called up his mother and asked her to lend him her little car. She readily agreed. He told Khyati they were going to his mother's house.

When he introduced Khyati to his mother, she seemed to take an immediate liking to the younger girl. She had to, for Khyati's cotton kurti matched her own saree.

As he watched the two of them chattering away, Avik realized that he had rarely seen Khyati wear revealing clothes, though he was sure a sexy body was concealed beneath the loose kurti.

She could make any sensible guy fall for her, he thought.

Avik soon excused himself and went to his room, leaving the duo to chat.

Thoughts about Khyati's body had made him miss Trisha. He missed the weight of her body on his own, but most of all he missed her smell. He had always been mesmerized by her tangy perfume. Even the thought of it still made him feel warm inside. But he knew that she was nothing more than an absent presence in his life, just as he was for her. She had not called him since they had last met, and neither had he made any effort to get in touch with her. He knew that Trisha was a closed chapter in his life. Right now all he wanted was Ananki Rajput's story.

If only he could discover the reason behind her current state of mind.

Madness is not something alien to human nature or reason but a part of it. There is a method to madness that cannot be seen by the ordinary eye. Madness is not cut off from reality. On the contrary, a mad person is submerged in reality, over-impassioned and highly susceptible to the outer world. A mad person is like a pearl without its shell, an animal without a skin and a stream without an ocean. Madness is not something that opposes rationality but a kind of superior reason, an insanity close to reason, Avik scribbled in his diary.

As he was jotting down his thoughts, he was called for dinner.

Avik smiled at the sight of the meal that had been laid out. For a moment he thought of settling down with Khyati and relishing such great meals every day for the rest of his life. But then he pulled the bridles of his mind's horses and laughed to himself at the thought.

As Khyati and his mother chatted away, a worrying thought suddenly occurred to him. He asked his mother for some homemade pickle, which she immediately went to fetch.

'Don't mention anything about Ananki's case to her,' Avik whispered.

'Avik, ever since we got here, I have not thought even once about the case. Don't worry about it,' Khyati whispered back.

Shakuntala returned with the pickle.

After dinner, Shakuntala insisted that the two of them stay the night as it was quite late. Khyati readily agreed and Avik soon returned to his room, leaving the two ladies to share their seemingly endless stories.

Avik struggled awake to check why his mobile was vibrating so early in the morning.

Khyati is calling me, but why, when she is in this house? he wondered. He answered the phone and said, 'The door is not locked—'

'Get ready and meet me at the government mental hospital at 11,' Khyati interrupted him. 'See you soon.' She hung up.

Avik looked at the clock. It was 10.10 a.m. already. He jumped out of bed and ran out of his room, calling out to his mother.

'Ma, where is Khyati?'

Ruchi Kokcha

'She left quite early in the morning, Avik. She said she had to meet someone urgently,' Shakuntala shouted back from the kitchen.

Avik got ready in a hurry, took his mother's car and sped to the government hospital where Dr Neerja was the head of the psychiatry department. Khyati was waiting for him at the entrance. He parked the car and they went inside.

4

The hospital was no less crowded and noisy than a fish market. They found it difficult to make their way through the corridor. There were people sitting on benches, while some, who were tired of standing while waiting for their turn, were either sitting or lying on the floor. A queer stench filled the place, a combination of sweat, medicines and floor cleaner.

Khyati covered her nose with her stole; her eyes were brimming because of the odour. It was nauseating. She clutched Avik's arm tightly so as not to lose him amidst the crowd. He walked quickly through the corridor, pulling her along. All of a sudden an adolescent boy in rags who was lying in the corridor grabbed Khyati's leg. Khyati tried hard to free herself, but his grip was tight. She started shouting for help. Avik tried to loosen the boy's grip, but could not do it by himself and called for help.

On hearing the commotion, two male attendants rushed to the spot to free Khyati while a female attendant went to call the doctor. As the three of them were trying to loosen the boy's grip, Avik saw the doctor come running. The nurse handed him an injection, which he quickly administered to the boy. A few minutes later the boy's grip loosened as he slowly lost consciousness. He was taken away to the male ward.

Avik noticed that Khyati was crying. He felt deeply grateful to her for all the trouble she was going to for his sake. He went up to her, wiped the tears from her cheeks, pulled her close and held her in his arms. When they continued down the corridor, Avik kept his arm around her shoulders to ensure that she was safe.

There weren't many people waiting outside Dr Neerja's room and they were soon sent in to see her. She was feeding a pair of goldfish and did not seem to notice Avik and Khyati as they entered. She was talking to the fish in a baby voice, just like a mother talks to an infant. The goldfish seemed to respond to her voice, as if they would jump out of the bowl straight into her hand. She turned around to find Avik and Khyati standing near her desk and asked them to take a seat. The baby voice was replaced by a serious tone.

'I went through Ananki's file. Strangely, the diagnosis and medications listed in the file are quite different from the ones in the referral letter written by Dr Kaul,' Dr Neerja told them.

'What do you mean, doctor?' asked Khyati, surprised.

'In the letter he says that she is suffering from serious histrionic personality disorder bordering on insanity. But according to her file, she suffered only from depression and anxiety in the initial stages. There is no record of any other psychological disorder,' she explained.

'You mean she was not mad,' Avik interrupted.

'It is worth noting that the dosage of antidepressants was steadily increased. Such high doses are never recommended, for they can cause severe addiction and withdrawal symptoms. She was also given neuroleptics, which are usually administered to people with a severe mental illness. It seems likely that her condition was aggravated.'

As she finished speaking, she placed Ananki's file in front of them. Avik gaped at the closed file for some time, struggling to speak.

'You mean to say that Dr Kaul intentionally gave her medication to make her condition worse?'

'It seems so,' Dr Neerja replied.

'But why would he want his patient to go crazy?' Khyati asked.

'He must have been told to do so by someone who wanted her to go mad,' Avik replied.

'Avik, I would advise you to stay out of it. Her father is a very powerful man. I have known Dr Kaul for many years and before today, I would never even have thought of challenging his diagnosis. Stay away from this case, you two. Go now,' Dr Neerja said as she stood up.

Avik and Khyati got up and left in silence.

Avik dropped Khyati off at the metro station before returning to his hotel room. It was difficult for him to accept the fact that he might not be able to complete the assignment for which he had left everything behind. Well, almost everything.

He stretched out on the couch and closed his eyes. He pictured Ananki Rajput, the girl next door.

Five days ago she had been just an old story. Now, her name haunted his consciousness.

Why is her story so important to me? Is it only because of the promotion I am expecting after this, the salary hike that will help me buy a new apartment to show off to my colleagues and friends? No. I can do without that. It is fame that I seek, being known to every single person, young or old, fame that will confer immortality upon me, so that my name lives on long after I am gone.

He knew he would not rest till he found out the truth behind Ananki's story.

He picked up his phone and texted Dr Neerja, requesting another meeting.

The next day he went to the Rajput family's bungalow in Civil Lines. He did not plan to meet Mr Rajput, given Dr Neerja's warning, but he hoped to meet Ananki's younger sister if her father was not at home. He told the guard that he was Ananki's friend and asked if he could see her. The guard looked at him suspiciously; clearly, the tactic had been used on him a hundred times before.

'The family has moved abroad,' he said and shut the gate in Avik's face.

Avik was not ready to give up so easily. He knew the guard was lying. As all the other threads of the story seemed out of his reach at the moment, Ananki's sister was the only one who might lead him further.

There is no other way, he thought, and decided to spy on the bungalow. On the morning of the fifth day, he saw three girls coming out of the premises. They got into a red Honda

City and left. Avik followed them to North Campus in his car. They parked the car opposite the Arts Faculty building. As they were walking to the building, Avik called out to them.

'Hey, please wait for me,' he shouted as he ran towards them.

The girls looked at him but did not stop, no doubt thinking that he was an eve-teaser or this was a prank being played on them by the boys from the Law Faculty.

Avik caught up with them before they entered the building.

'Please. I beg of you. Wait. It is a matter of someone's life. Stop, please,' he said as he gasped for breath.

Seeing his troubled countenance, one of them decided to listen to him.

'All right. We have to submit some papers, but meet us at the Vivekananda statue in half an hour,' the girl said, pointing to a black statue standing directly behind him.

Avik stood out in the sun, waiting. It had been almost two hours since the girls had entered the Arts Faculty building and there was still no sign of them. Avik wondered if there was another exit in the building, if they had fooled him. After all, why should they come back to help him; they did not even know him. As these doubts ran through his mind, he saw the girl who had spoken to him waving at him. She was extremely beautiful, though not very tall, probably not more than 5'4". Quite fit and with an attractive figure, she was definitely a head-turner. Avik quickly walked up to her.

'Sorry for being late, but it can take forever to make submissions.'

'What are you studying?' Avik asked as they waited for the other two girls to join them.

'We are doing our master's in English literature, final year. I am Priyanka, and these are my friends, Sarika and Hetal,' the girl said as her friends walked up to them.

Avik realized that she was Ananki's sister.

He introduced himself to the three girls, shaking hands with each of them, holding Priyanka's soft hand for a little longer than he held the others'.

'I don't mean to trouble you, but I need your help in a really important matter. It would be great if we could go someplace where we can sit and talk and I can have something to drink,' Avik pleaded.

The girls seemed hesitant, but agreed to go with him to Hudson Lane in Kamla Nagar. They sat in a rickshaw and Avik followed them in another one.

Hudson Lane had many memories associated with it for Avik. *It has always been a mecca for collegegoers. It offers cheap food and drinks and is a blessing for young lovers who don't want to wander around in the Delhi Ridge area surrounding campus*, Avik recollected as the rickshaws reached Hudson Lane.

They selected a restaurant and after they had ordered drinks, Priyanka asked Avik why he wanted to talk to them.

'I am a journalist, working on a very important case. I have no intention of harming you or getting you into trouble,' Avik said in an attempt to win her trust.

'What have we to do with this case of yours?' Priyanka asked.

'Do you know Ananki Rajput?'he asked.

At this Priyanka stood up and left like a bullet, without a word. Avik had caught a glimpse of the grief on her face. He rushed after her.

'Are you Ananki's sister?' he asked, catching hold of her wrist.

She shrugged his hand off and phoned her chauffeur as she continued walking towards the main road. Avik followed her, reiterating that it was important for him to learn more about Ananki.

'Why is this important to you? Who are you to her? A family member? Relative? Friend? Who? Yes, I am her sister. If I can survive a life without her, then anyone can. What difference does it make to you if she is living or dead or if she is stuck somewhere in the middle?' Priyanka howled at him. Passersby stared at them, making Avik a little uncomfortable.

Avik was stunned by the extent of her fury. He kept mum as he followed her to her car, which had just pulled up, but as she opened the door, he asked her to listen to him for one last time.

'I am nothing to her. But she has become someone to me. I have never seen her, but her presence holds my mind and constantly pushes me to seek her out in the real world. It might sound insane to you, but this is my truth, and in turn I would like the same from you,' Avik said earnestly.

Priyanka noticed how casually he used the word 'insane'.

'If only you really knew what being insane is like. It is a double-layered mirrored box that isolates the one locked inside from the rest of the world. The outer world can only see its own reflection while the person locked inside can see his or her own self, a self behind another self till infinity, each different from its predecessor, making it impossible for the one caught inside to choose one self over another,' Priyanka had tears in her eyes as she said this, and she held on to the open car door. She took a deep breath before continuing, 'What if, in such a dilemma, one loses oneself? Gives up on every self that one sees? Is that what insanity is?'

Not knowing what to say, Avik remained silent.

She looked at him, and then seemed to come to a decision.

'Meet me tomorrow at the same place. I will come only for a short period of time, as I am not allowed to stay out for long,' she said.

'Can I have your phone number?' he asked.

She got inside the car without replying to him and asked the chauffeur to drive away. He quickly wrote his number on a piece of paper and threw it inside the open window of the car. She rolled up the window as the car vanished in a cloud of dust.

Priyanka did not turn up the next day. Her friend Hetal came to inform Avik that Priyanka could not leave the house, nor could she make a phone call, for her father was keeping a close eye on her outings.

'He has become very strict after the tragedy at home,' Hetal told him.

Avik led Hetal to a cement bench so they could sit and talk.

'What tragedy?' he inquired.

'Priyanka's sister seems to have lost it completely because of some past trauma and her mother's death. That is all I know. The entire family broke to pieces. Anyway, I have to leave, but Priyanka said she would meet you tomorrow at this same spot,' she replied.

Avik stood up and walked with her to her car.

That evening he got a call from Sahay asking about his progress with the case.

'I am uncovering information bit by bit. It's a lot more complicated than we ever imagined it to be and will require more time and patience.'

Avik thought it better not to inform Sahay about Dr Neerja's warning. He would likely be called back empty-handed and Sahay would make sure to keep him busy with some mundane assignment.

'What about the new apartment?' Avik tried to divert Sahay's attention from the case.

'You will be moved soon, don't worry about that. Just concentrate on what's been given to you,' Sahay said quickly and hung up.

Avik wanted to remain in Delhi and find Ananki. For a moment, he felt that the journalist in him had died; he no longer cared if the story was published or not. All that mattered to him was Ananki's story. No matter how far he travelled away from it, he would somehow always return to her story.

Her phantasm in my subconscious will haunt me till I reach her in the real world, Avik thought as he drifted asleep.

The following day, he reached the meeting point at the appointed hour. He was relieved to see that Priyanka was waiting for him. 'I'm happy you could make it today. But how did you manage to come here today and not yesterday?'

'I am sorry for not turning up yesterday. I had a submission to make today so I could meet you. Dad keeps a check on everything I do, you see,' she replied as she put her heavy bag down on the ground. 'Shall we hurry up? It's too hot here,' she prompted him.

Avik looked at her overstuffed bag.

'Are you planning to run away?' he asked.

'I am not running away, I'm making you run away with someone.'

'Ah, I see! Who is the lucky girl, if I may know?' He chuckled.

'Ananki,' Priyanka replied and took out a fountain pen, a black diary, a photo album, a pocketbook of Shakespeare's sonnets, a mouth organ and a chequered scarf from the bag. She handed them all to him.

'That's all I have of hers. Go now, before anyone sees you with these things. I can't stay, but all these things will direct you to her.'

'Look, I am sorry for not saying anything earlier, but I should have given you my condolences the day before. Will you accept them today?' Avik asked Priyanka as he placed the objects on the bench.

Priyanka could only nod at him in answer.

He read the sadness in her eyes. It was certainly not a good time to ask her, but he had no choice. He knew he might never see her again.

'Priyanka, will you pardon me if I ask you what you think about your mom's death? Do you think she met with an accident? Or did she have some problems because of which she committed suicide?'

'She had no problems at all. She had everything a woman could wish for – a successful career, a great family and a doting husband who would do, and did, anything and everything to make her happy. Her death was definitely not a suicide. She just could not have done such a thing,' Priyanka replied in a low voice.

'Then you believe it was murder?' Avik asked.

'No. No. I did not mean that. As far as I know, she did not have any personal or professional rivalries. Even her competitors admired her. They were part of her social circle. Why would anyone want to kill her? I cannot think of a reason. Maybe it was an accident. Yes, it must have been an accident. It was fate that a woman so dynamic had so little time.'

'Okay. Do you know anyone who could give me more information on her professional life? Maybe her personal assistant or someone who worked closely with her?' Avik asked.

'I am not sure. If I find out, I will text you the information. I cannot stay any longer. Bye,' Priyanka said as she hurried to her car.

Avik watched the car till it was lost to sight, and then directed his attention to the things Priyanka had given him.

He picked up the fountain pen. It had a black-and-gold body.

Very classy. It must be an expensive pen, he thought.

He pulled off the cap to find a shiny gold nib with 'Waterman Paris' engraved on it. He placed the cap on the back of the pen, picked up the book of sonnets, turned to the last page and wrote Ananki's name on it.

Although he could not boast of having great handwriting, he had written her name out carefully, in the style of a calligraphic inscription.

He was lost in the beauty of it. *Ananki*, he whispered to himself.

5

Avik sat cross-legged on the bed, the pen, the photo album, the diary, the book of sonnets, the mouth organ and the scarf laid out in front of him.

He picked up the photo album. It was a scrapbook made by Ananki herself. On the cover she had written *'The Chronicle of My Life'* in red ink.

Her handwriting is so beautiful, Avik observed as he moved his fingertips over the writing.

In the top left corner of the cover was painted a peacock feather. A golden-yellow lace border made the cover look very attractive.

How artistic, he thought and turned the cover to look at the first page. It had pictures of Ananki as a baby, each with a little caption. In one of them, her mother and father both held her. Something strange caught his eye.

He flipped through the pages quickly and noticed that several photographs had scratches in black ink across them.

The marks, however, did not appear to be the work of a child inadvertently scribbling on the pages.

These look deliberate. In every picture in which her mother and father were with Ananki, the image of her mother had been crossed out, her face besmirched with black ink. *What can it mean?* Avik wondered as he took out his handkerchief and went to the bathroom.

Avik wetted his handkerchief and used it to try and rub off the ink stains from one of the pictures. He could not clean it – the marker was permanent. He then tried to remove the marks with acetone.

It helped to some extent, but the face was so badly scored with scratch marks that it looked as if it had been mutilated by an axe and not a pen. It was frightening to behold. He closed the album with a snap.

I guess my mind is overcrowded with all sorts of thoughts. I should rest for a while.

He cleared the bed of Ananki's belongings, switched off the lights and lay down. As he closed his eyes, the mutilated face of Ananki's mother flashed through his mind. Keeping his eyes open appeared a better option to him, and he gazed unblinkingly at the empty ceiling in the dark room. Only a ray of street light peeped in through the little gap between the two curtains.

Avik did not know when the ceiling changed colour from dark grey to pearl white.

A dreamless sleep always refreshed him. He woke up feeling much better than he had the previous night, ordered tea and breakfast and went for a shower. When he came out of the bathroom, the tea and sandwiches were laid out on the coffee table. He picked up a cup of tea and went to fetch the album, which was lying on the bedside table. He looked at the photos and the captions more carefully. *The markings get deeper and darker as Ananki grows older.* The last photo had been taken on Ananki's fourteenth birthday; her father (and mother) were standing on either side of her, kissing her on each cheek. But one could hardly see her mother. She had been blacked out almost completely.

What could possibly be the cause of such a strong reaction? It appears that Ananki did not want to see her mother's face, as if seeing her reminded her of something, or brought alive the pain associated with her death.

After much contemplation, Avik concluded that it could have been the trauma of losing her mother that had made Ananki react in such a manner.

Losing someone we love can create a great void in the mind and losing someone as important as one's mother can make the void even deeper. Remembrance can be heart-rending. Memories can become a source of perpetual pain and remind one of the loss. When we lose someone we love, our first reaction is to bury the memories associated with the person so that they do not trouble us. Scratching out her mother's images may have been Ananki's way of stopping the pain caused by memories. But can the memories associated with a lost loved one really be erased from our minds? Are memories not a way to keep a loved one alive in our consciousness?

Contemplating Ananki's loss, Avik recalled the day when he had lost his father. His father had had a huge circle of friends, unlike Avik. The day he died, people from all spheres of his life—relatives, friends and colleagues—had come to bid him farewell.

Avik had cried a lot, knowing that the man he had looked up to all his life would no longer be present behind him. The hand that had been placed firmly on his back in times of his failures and on his shoulder when he succeeded would no longer be there for him. The death of a parent can cause a black hole in one's life. One moment you stand safe between the foundation below and the marquee above you, and the next moment one of them tragically disappears from your life forever. Avik put the album down and closed his glistening eyes as he thought about his father.

He realized that death is not the source of one's pain. The memories associated with the person and the fact that the memories can never be brought to life are more tormenting.

As Avik sat on the chair staring at Ananki's belongings, he began to feel restless. He realized that he was not content with the conclusion he had jumped to. Something didn't seem right.

Could she really have been so aggressive in dealing with her mother's absence, or was there something else on her mind that made her cross out Kalki's pictures one after the other?

He picked up the album once more and looked at the markings. On careful observation he saw that the ink marks were of different colours. The ones in the initial photographs were lighter than the ones in the later pictures. Avik was perplexed.

Had the act been a device to cope with her mother's death, all of the ink marks would have been of the same colour, if not the same intensity. It is as if the marks on each photograph are as old as the photograph itself. Avik noticed that the marks on the older photographs had faded over time while those on the more recent photographs appeared fresher.

They do not appear to be an abrupt reaction caused by Kalki's death, but a conscious deed performed over a period of time. Maybe they are an expression of a childhood trauma wherein her mother became a source of an unending anguish; perhaps she favoured her sister over her and this was Ananki's way of erasing the pain, Avik conjectured.

Lack of love from someone close to you can play havoc in one's mind. Indeed, Kalki's behaviour could be the reason behind Ananki's mental condition.

Satisfied with the conclusion he had reached, Avik put down the album and picked up the book of sonnets. It was an old book, dated 1609, with a blue hardbound cover.

Avik opened the book, holding one of the pages between his thumb and index finger, feeling the stiff, yellowish-brown paper. He lifted the book to his nose and inhaled the exotic, earthy fragrance that ensorcelled him. He flipped through the book twice, from cover to cover, and in doing so, discovered that the corner of one of the pages had been folded in. He opened the book to the page and read the heading: 'Sonnet 142'. He read the first line, 'Love is my sin and thy dear virtue hate', and then read the entire sonnet. He could not understand Shakespeare's language. He had never read much English literature, preferring popular fiction and bestsellers whenever he found the time to read. He resorted to Google to decipher what the sonnet conveyed. After reading a few articles that explained Shakespeare to amateurs like him, he opened Ananki's book to the page with Sonnet 142.

Why is this sonnet marked? Is it her favourite sonnet in the collection or is it the last one she read? Questions invaded his mind.

Avik picked up the chequered scarf and wrapped it around his neck in the classic Dev Anand style. He picked up the mouth organ and went to the mirror to have a look at himself. As he blew into the mouth organ, his lips curved into a smile at his 1960s image.

Everything about Ananki is so classy. When one has the money to spend on the most desirable of things, why would one not do it? But then these are not things that a rich girl would normally spend her money on. Indeed she is different, very different from most people of her class. Only her own words can throw light on who she really is.

Lost in thoughts of Ananki, Avik walked towards the bedside table to get the diary but stumbled on the uneven floor and fell. He cut his forehead on the corner of the coffee table, barely sparing his eye. Shaken, he stood up and called the reception to ask for a bandage.

After washing the wound with cold water, he covered it with the bandage. He cursed himself several times, took a painkiller and lay on the bed.

Is this a sign that I should step back from this case? Why does it get more and more complicated each day, making me dive deeper and deeper into it? Should I stop and tell Sahay that this unknown ocean will never be fathomed? What if I'm wasting my time on this story? Is it all worth it?

Avik's drowsy mind had become a battleground of questions. He did not know when sleep rescued him from the war. He woke up a few hours later to find it was already evening. He checked his mobile. Khyati had called him twice in the afternoon. He called her back and told her about the accident.

'Oh my goodness! Are you all right?' she sounded worried.

'Yes, I am fine now.'

'But why didn't you call me? Do you not consider me to be your friend?'

'It is not like that, Khyati. I did not want to bother you for a little bruise. I am man enough to handle things like that.'

Khyati sensed the agitation in his voice.

'I know you can take care of yourself, but sometimes the presence of a friend helps. I am going to come over. No more discussion,' she said and hung up.

On the way, Khyati had some food packed from the dhaba near Avik's hotel. Avik had many a times praised the aroma that came from the dhaba. She knew good food would help lift his spirits.

She was right; Avik smiled as soon as he opened the door and smelt the food. He had been dying of hunger ever since he had woken up, but it had not occurred to him to order something to eat. He pounced on the aromatic bag Khyati held in her hand and within no time was gorging on butter chicken and naan. Khyati smiled to see him eating with his hands, not bothering about the mess he made.

Serenity returned to Avik as he finished his meal and washed his hands. He pulled up a chair beside Khyati's and directed her attention to the objects on the table.

Khyati knew immediately who the things belonged to. 'I see you managed to extort things from the witch's own warehouse,' she said.

'Don't call her a witch. She is just a person, like you and me, only she has excluded herself from our world and made another one for herself. Normal people like you and me who live by reason cannot comprehend what it is like to live like her,' Avik defended Ananki, surprising Khyati.

'I did not mean it that way. I understand how it is. I am studying psychology, after all. I was only joking. Now forget it and tell me how you were able to get these things.'

Avik told her how he had met Priyanka and that she had given him Ananki's things. As Avik was speaking, Khyati realized that he was willing to risk his life and career for this story.

'Why has this become so important for you, Avik?' she finally asked him.

'I feel that knowing Ananki's story is crucial to me, as if it's a quest to know myself,' Avik replied after a long silence.

Khyati feared that Avik was trapped in Ananki's story. He could only disentangle himself once he had cut the cords that bound him, and she would do anything to pull him out of it. Khyati's thoughts were interrupted by a phone call from Dr Tarun.

'I have to leave now,' she said.

'I thought you were going to stay tonight,' he replied.

'No, I forgot I have to complete a case study. Dr Tarun just reminded me about it. I should go.'

Khyati had lied. She always completed her work before it was due. But although she had initially planned to spend the night at the hotel, after their conversation, she no longer wanted to stay. She thought it would be better to leave Avik alone so that he could contemplate where his life was heading.

Dr Tarun's call reminded Avik that Dr Neerja had never responded to his message about meeting Ananki. He asked Khyati to phone the doctor and set up a meeting for the following day. Though Khyati was quite reluctant to call Dr Neerja on Avik's behalf, he was adamant, saying he would not let her leave until she made the call.

Khyati gave in and called Dr Neerja. However, although she tried hard to convince her to set up a meeting, Dr Neerja did not agree. Seeing that Khyati was unable to persuade her, Avik took the phone from her and told the doctor about his meeting with Priyanka, and getting Ananki's belongings. He suspected that Dr Neerja would want to see Ananki's things. He was right; she could not pass up the opportunity to learn more about Ananki's background, which she had been looking into with little success. She agreed to meet them at her home the next morning.

Avik felt more confident after the call. He knew Dr Neerja would be able to piece together the scattered pieces of the jigsaw.

Little did he know that sometimes the logical, critical eye fails to look beyond a point, a point that marks the end of the realm of reason and the beginning of another world. A world where one has to leave logic at the door before one enters it. Only those who can look beyond reason and common sense can pass the 'reason extermination' test, which dismisses all reason, for only they dare to enter the long maze that follows. If there was anyone who could pass the test, it was Avik, though he did not know it yet.

Khyati picked up her bag to leave but Avik stopped her.

'Tell me honestly, do you really have work pending?' he asked, blocking her way.

'No. But I can't stay,' Khyati replied, trying to go past him.

'You cannot leave me. I want you to help me. You are the one person whom I can talk to about this case. I was not defending Ananki. I was just trying to empathize. I thought you would understand. Please stay with me.' Avik reached out to hold her hand, melting Khyati's caring heart.

Khyati put her bag back on the table, sat down on a chair and looked through Ananki's belongings one by one, picking up the diary last. Avik lit a cigarette and sat next to her so he could look at the diary with her. It could not be opened, as it was locked by a clasp with a numeric code. Khyati tried a few combinations, followed by Avik, but none of them worked.

'Only Ananki can open the diary and for that to happen, it is necessary that she agrees to meet me,' Avik said.

'We can break the lock, can't we?' Khyati suggested, keeping the diary back on the table.

'Breaking the lock would mean losing Ananki's trust forever. She might never talk to me, and her opening up is crucial to know her story in her own words. The time for speculations and assumptions has to be left behind for reality to come forth,' he replied, picking up the diary.

He tried to peep into the pages by pulling the covers apart, but the diary was tightly bound and it was difficult to make space between the pages. He did not give up, however. His effort paid off as he saw that something had been kept between the pages, a folded piece of paper.

Avik shook the diary several times in an attempt to dislodge the paper, but it was wedged in tight.

'Do you have a nail file or a hairpin?' he asked Khyati.

She searched in her bag and found a pair of tweezers. Avik took them from her and pushed them in slowly between the pages of the diary. Khyati pulled at the sides of the diary to help Avik ease the paper out. It was a pink sheet, folded over once. Avik quickly unfolded it.

'It's a letter. How can you read someone else's letter?' Khyati exclaimed.

He merely stared at her and, without replying, looked at the letter. It was written in deep red ink, with a thick-nibbed pen, in calligraphy.

For a moment Avik just wondered at the beauty of the writing. He felt as if the unknown red words had enchanted him. He gazed at the words without reading them, and then handed the letter to Khyati who read it silently at first and then, on Avik's request, read it aloud.

Dear Da,
This is the first time that I'm writing to you. It is not possible for me to hide from you the sea of emotions

that surge within me every night and day. It is also strange to me how you hold such a position in my life, despite being 'You'. I do not remember when I started feeling like this about you, taking your hugs and kisses as tokens of passion when I knew you did not have the same level of feelings for me. To think about you as I should is something that I cannot do, no matter how hard I try; it has gone much beyond my control. I'm not mad, but if I express my passion for you freely, I would definitely be called insane. But is that not what love is? Love is beyond logical explanations. I cannot give any reason as to why and how I developed such feelings for you despite knowing the nature of our relationship. I have always loved you, ever since I learnt what the love of a woman for a man is. You are the only man in my life and this equation will not change, come what may. I have many more confessions to make. Please meet me once, alone, anywhere you say.

I love you so much.

Yours only
A.

Khyati handed the letter back to Avik. He happened to hold it exactly where Ananki had left a kiss for the addressee. The lipstick mark was still visible.

'Any idea to whom this letter is addressed?' she asked.

Avik had no clue who the man was, but it was clear to them that it was someone whom Ananki had known for a very long time, a childhood friend perhaps, someone close to her, someone she was not 'supposed' to love but she did.

The contents of the letter disturbed Avik, making him yearn for solitude. He no longer wanted Khyati to stay with him. He wanted her to leave so that he could hold the letter close to his chest, as if the words in it would seep through his skin and reach his bloodstream, infusing perfectly to flow through his veins.

'I feel like going for a long walk,' Avik said to Khyati, hinting that she should leave.

He quickly called her a cab, then walked with her to the main road. When the cab arrived, he gave her an almost reluctant hug.

'I'll see you at Dr Neerja's place tomorrow,' Khyati said as she sat in the cab. He nodded and waved at her.

Avik ran back to his hotel room as fast as he could. Khyati turned around to watch him through the rear window of the cab. Seeing Avik running back towards the hotel like a bullet, she realized that something was affecting him deeply, making him behave strangely.

This is certainly not a good sign, she thought.

Avik reached his room, struggling to catch his breath. He drank the entire contents of the jug lying on the bedside table. Feeling relieved, he picked up the letter and looked at it again, reading what the beautifully written red words said. He read the letter in its entirety first. Then in the second go he read each word with a distinct pause, as if it was independent, not part of a sentence.

'Each word is so wondrous to behold,' he whispered, moving his finger over each of them.

His finger went to the bottom of the letter to feel the spot where her lips had left their mark. He brought the letter close to his face and breathed in deeply. He kissed the mark in a daze, then licked it. The act hardened him. He lay down on his bed, the letter covering his face, and let his hands reach down to caress himself.

He woke up the next morning to find himself naked, the letter lying on his left. He paused to think whether last night's act should fill him with shame.

I have worked with a lot of female colleagues, but never fantasized about any of them. It's not that I never thought about a woman while easing myself, but never like this. How could I have fantasized about a woman without knowing or seeing her in person, enticed just by the mark left by her lips?

6

Avik got ready and left for Dr Neerja's house. On the way he thought about why the letter had had such a gripping effect on him.

Ananki is permeating my self almost to the point of controlling my instincts. The thought sent a shiver down his spine. *It is time that I snap this strange connection and gain greater command over my actions.*

When he arrived at Dr Neerja's home, he saw that Khyati was already there, talking to her as they sat at a tea table in the garden. Dr Neerja was looking at her seriously, making notes as Khyati spoke.

Avik felt betrayed and walked briskly towards the table, calling out a greeting so as to interrupt their conversation. Dr Neerja turned to him and then smiled when she saw the bag he carried. She left the two together and went into the house to bring tea for Avik.

Avik sat silently on the chair beside Khyati, not looking at her even once, which bothered her. She asked him why he was behaving so strangely. Avik tried hard to push his anger down, ignoring her for some time, then blurted out, 'Why did you have to discuss Ananki's belongings before I got here? Could you not wait? Or maybe you just wanted to take all the credit for yourself? I never thought you would do this to me.'

Khyati was stunned at this bombardment. For the first time she regretted helping him with this case. Her eyes were full of anger and with great effort, she forced a reply to Avik's accusations.

'I feel sorry for you, Avik, for thinking such things about me. I was talking to Dr Neerja about the therapies that should be used in cases where the patient does not respond to any external stimuli, like Ananki, who has shut herself off from the outer world. I wanted to help you, but I don't think you deserve it. All the best for this and your future endeavours.'

Avik noticed that although her voice was low, it was brimming with anger, as if she were grinding her teeth. She got up and walked away without waiting for Dr Neerja to return. Feeling contrite, Avik went after her. He caught hold of her hand and asked for forgiveness. He found it difficult to explain what had seized him, making him say the things he did.

Khyati knew something was affecting him more and more with each passing day. She did not feel right leaving him alone in such a state. So for everything she had always felt for him, she returned to her chair and sat down.

When Dr Neerja returned with Avik's tea, she sensed that something had happened in her absence, but she did not question either of the two, for things of greater importance were awaiting her attention.

Avik narrated how he had met Priyanka and thus taken a step further towards Ananki.

Dr Neerja looked at Ananki's belongings one by one, scrutinizing each in silence, seemingly unaware of her audience. She read the letter, removed her reading glasses, and looked up at Avik and Khyati. She cleared her throat and addressed them in a serious tone.

'I had always thought this girl was very different from others and looking at these things, I believe I was not wrong. It seems she was very artistic. It can only be speculated from these articles that unrequited love followed by her mother's death could have led her to her present condition. Since you two have helped so much with this case, I would like to share that personally, I don't think things are going well with her and her silence makes me feel helpless. She prefers to remain locked in her closet, not letting anyone help her,' Dr Neerja said, looking only at Avik as she spoke the last sentence.

Avik listened to her with unblinking attention. When she finished, he asked her again, 'Can I see her once?'

Dr Neerja shook her head, but Avik pleaded with her to let him meet Ananki. She could see his desperation but did not understand the reason behind it. To find out more, she would have to agree to his request.

'Only once.' Dr Neerja asked him to accompany her to her NGO, which was where Ananki was being kept.

Khyati could not go with them, as she had to assist Dr Bhalla that afternoon. She did not want Avik to go alone, but she knew that he would not wait for another day for her sake. So she merely waved to him as he sat in Dr Neerja's car and vanished in a cloud of dust.

He did not even say bye, Khyati thought frowning. She was disappointed and felt it was better to stay away from him as much as possible. Indifference was something she could not tolerate from him, especially in light of all the help she was giving him.

'What makes you so interested in Ananki's case?' Dr Neerja asked Avik on the way to the NGO.

Avik felt a sense of shame, as if she had a window into his mind and could see what he had done last night.

'I am just curious to learn the reason behind her madness,' he managed to answer, looking down.

Dr Neerja was not very satisfied with his reply, but she did not probe him further. She thought it better to prepare Avik for what was to come, as she was sure he never had, and never would again, experience what he was about to witness at the NGO.

'You have to be strong, Avik. Keeping a check on your emotions while you are watching her is important. You may see some disturbing things, but make sure you don't let them affect you. It should just be a case for you. Do not attach your empathy to it,' Dr Neerja warned, stressing the word 'empathy'.

When they reached the NGO, Dr Neerja told Avik to wait in her office while she went to check on Ananki. He looked tense as he waited. Dr Neerja had given him strict instructions not to say anything or make his presence known when he saw Ananki. *One mistake and we might lose the chance of bringing her out of her closet forever*, he thought, his eyes fixed on the door as he waited anxiously for the doctor to return.

After waiting for about two hours, Avik was finally summoned by Dr Neerja. He was wearing a black shirt and khaki pants. He pulled out Ananki's chequered scarf from the bag containing her belongings and wore it around his neck, just like he had the other day.

The nurse who had come to get him led him down a corridor to a flight of stairs leading to the basement. The corridor was poorly lit and not very clean. It appeared from the dust that covered the floor that it was hardly used. As he walked down the stairs to the basement, the light diminished with every step he took, till it was almost dark. He extended his hand, sliding it along the wall as he continued down the stairs. He could feel the dust and the rough cement against his palm as he stepped down, one by one, wholly by instinct. On the second-last step, he felt a spiderweb brush against his face. 'What the hell!' Avik exclaimed, waving his hands around in front of his face in an attempt to get rid of it.

The nurse hushed him.

Avik stepped into a corridor lit with a single bulb that hardly threw any light. The place was repulsive to him. He could not understand why someone would prefer to stay in a place like this.

As if reading his mind, the nurse whispered, 'She prefers to stay in the dark. She grows more violent when we keep her in the bright rooms, or in the backyard, making it difficult for the other patients. Here in this basement she lies as quietly as a lizard on a wall, unmoving and blind to everything else.'

She pointed out a room at the end of the corridor, hardly five steps from where he stood, before leaving him.

As he approached the room, which had a door made of iron bars, he heard someone coming down the stairs. An attendant had brought food for Ananki.

Dr Neerja signalled to the attendant to put the tray of food inside the cell. She then led Avik to a room opposite Ananki's cell. It had a wooden door with a small viewing panel at eye-level so one could observe what went on in the cell opposite. He could only watch Ananki from inside this room. Dr Neerja placed her forefinger on her lips, giving him a sign not to make the slightest of sounds or show himself. Avik gave her a thumbs up to assure her that he would follow her instructions.

The attendant had placed the tray of food on the floor of Ananki's cell and locked the door behind him. He and Dr Neerja left, leaving Avik and Ananki opposite each other in the dark. While he was trying hard to make out what was happening in the room behind the bars, someone switched on a dim light, making the girl inside in the dark groan. He could now see her facing the wall opposite the barred door, scribbling something on it with a piece of black chalk, charcoal perhaps.

He remembered being told earlier by Dr Neerja that this was Ananki's favourite activity. He could not believe that someone could be so adept at writing in complete darkness.

Over time her eyes must have become accustomed to writing in the dark. It's as if she herself does not want to see what she writes, he mused.

Avik stared through the viewing panel not just to look at Ananki but also to spare himself from the darkness that surrounded him. The only darkness he ever trusted was the one inside him, but this darkness outside was alien to him.

His mind was torn apart amidst the darkness, both the inner one and the outer one, the two battling against each other. The only thing that could help him was the sight of Ananki. He cupped his hands on either side of his face, shielding his eyes from the darkness outside and focusing on the figure opposite him.

Long black curls kissed her thighs and swayed as her lean hands moved briskly across the wall, both of them simultaneously, as if in a hurry to finish. She moved quickly from left to right on her toes, never once letting her heels touch the ground. Her sheer white gown barely covered her knees, exposing her thin calves. The fragile frame proved her distaste for food. In contrast to her slight figure was her long, luxurious hair. What nourished it to grow to such a length was a mystery; it was as if her hair was the only part of her that was alive.

While he was caught up in watching her, he felt something move over his feet, a rat perhaps. He shuffled his feet in fear, not of the rat, but of the darkness that engulfed him. The sound startled her, making her drop both hands to her sides, each one still holding a piece of charcoal. He cursed himself for diverting her attention. She turned to look at the tray of food, perhaps to make sure that a rat was not eating out of it, and he was able to see her profile. He looked at her face and felt frozen in the moment, a feeling of déjà vu overcoming him.

I have seen her before. Avik could not place where and how, for this was the first time he was seeing her in person. *She bears no resemblance to the Ananki Rajput in the photographs I saw a few days back.*

She was wearing a silver nose ring that glowed like a crescent moon on her sharp nose. Her long neck, which protruded between prominent collarbones, looked strange; he had the eerie feeling that she could rotate it 360 degrees. Her sheer gown did nothing to conceal her nipples, which tipped small, worn-out breasts.

I have seen it all before – that face, those breasts and those locks. She resembles the half-serpent, half-woman I saw in my dream, he gasped in sudden realization.

Avik closed his eyes at once, not daring to look at her any longer. The figure from his dream flashed before him, her hair a writhing mass of snakes, their venomous jaws opened wide. The figure smiled treacherously at him and created a clone of the girl in the cell. She held the clone's hand and drew her close, hugging her. The serpent woman's writhing hair pecked at each and every part of the clone's body. Gradually, the two merged into a single feminine being, Sernanki.

The merging released a blinding flash of light and Sernanki grew in size, revealing four hands, two on either side, four breasts, two with red nipples and two with black, the large areola of each wrinkled with snake skin. She had two navels, one sunk in and the other protruding out. Beneath the protruding navel was visible a red pudendum, out of which grew endless red serpents. Below the other navel was a black pudendum. She had two legs and a tail.

Within no time she grew to fill the cell. The roof exploded to make space for her, but she did not stop growing. He could see her reach the sky, beyond the limits of what could be seen by the human eye. She was floating over a blue egg. The long red snakes coiled around the egg, as if to hatch it.

Suddenly, one of the red snakes, larger than the rest, noticed him. It swooped at him and, picking him up in its jaws, sped towards the sky. It stopped before the red pudendum and he was sucked in amidst a hurricane of fire. Sernanki roared with laughter. Her final victorious howl was louder than the thunder of the thickest of clouds. She now possessed him forever.

Avik was drenched in sweat. He had just envisioned himself being ingurgitated and he feared that the girl opposite him might also lead to his annihilation.

He mustered the courage to look out at Ananki once more. She was eating, pushing her locks away to keep them from the plate. Her eyebrows were joined together above her nose, like two baby snakes that had discovered the joy of kissing. Her eyes were too big for her small face. Her lips were dry and trembling as if with the weight of her upper lip, which had not been plucked of its hair in a long time.

She stood up to keep the empty plate outside the door so the attendant would not have to enter her cell. He could now see her clearly.

Either she is quite tall or her lean frame makes her look taller, Avik noticed.

Her legs were covered with fine hair that grew darker at the crotch, making it more prominent under the sheer white gown. From her deep navel, a trail of hair travelled towards her crotch, like a stream searching for a release in the dark sea. Her barely concealed body was a captivating sight for him, not because of its near nakedness, but because it was so natural.

I have never seen such raw sexuality. Every woman I have seen has been plucked, waxed, polished and made perfect for the man she seeks, but she is the first one I have come across who unknowingly celebrates her natural feminine sexuality without the objective of finding an admirer, he thought, bewitched.

To him she appeared as an infant, completely in harmony with her natural body, knowing nothing artificial or fake. Her raw beauty made him forget the phantasm of self-destruction that had seized his mind and body just a few minutes ago.

Avik's reverie was interrupted by the attendant who had returned to collect the food tray. After he picked it up, he turned to Avik and motioned for him to follow him.

Avik did not want to leave, but he knew he had no choice. He opened the door of his room and without making a sound, went and stood in front of Ananki's cell. He could not see her, which caused him great despair. He pulled her scarf from around his neck and tied it to one of the bars before leaving, in the hope that she might at least know he had been there.

As he climbed up the stairs he wondered if she would recognize the scarf, whether it would lead him to her once more or if this was all he could have of her.

If only I could see her one more time it would be enough for me.

He went to Dr Neerja's room. She was having lunch and asked if he wanted to join her. Avik had no desire to eat; somehow he felt full despite not having eaten anything since that morning. He courteously declined and sat silently as Dr Neerja finished her meal.

As she ate, the doctor observed the tumult that was clearly going on in Avik's mind. He looked pale and sick. Suddenly, he got up to leave. Dr Neerja asked him to sit down. She wanted him to talk about his experience of seeing Ananki.

Avik remained silent for a few minutes and then burst into tears. Dr Neerja was startled. She had not expected such a response from him. Avik regained his composure quickly, but hated himself for exposing his emotionally fragile and vulnerable side.

'Are all patients kept in such a state?' he finally asked her.

'No, the other patients are kept in the general ward. It is she who has chosen such a life for herself, away from light, away from life. It is strange to see a person with her background give up everything and go back to a primal state of existence. At first she even gave up clothing and other basic necessities.

The nurses would have a tough time bathing her. Sometimes she would not have a bath for days. She would tear apart the clothes they put on her. It was only after much counselling that she finally agreed to wear a gown.'

Avik stood and picked up the bag containing Ananki's belongings. He took out the mouth organ.

'When can I meet her?' he reiterated his question.

'You cannot meet her,' the doctor replied, pressing her lips together, giving him a grim, hopeless look.

Avik nodded and left the room, but he could not give up so easily. On the way out of the NGO he saw the attendant who had brought food for Ananki. He looked around and then went up to him, inviting him for a cup of tea and a smoke at the stall outside the NGO.

Avik sensed that Dr Neerja would not be of much help in this case. He had to take another course.

Sonu, the attendant, joined Avik at the tea stall. Avik told him that he wanted to meet Ananki but Dr Neerja might not let him.

'Dr Neerja is particularly careful about her. She visits her every day. If you want to meet her, it has to be on a day when she is at the hospital or out for meetings,' Sonu said.

'Will you keep a check on Dr Neerja and help me meet Ananki as soon as possible?' Avik asked, trying hard to hide the desperation in his tone.

'Yes, but it involves a lot of risk. If caught, I might lose my job.' Sonu was smart enough to read the urgency in Avik's eyes.

For five thousand rupees, the attendant agreed to deliver the mouth organ to Ananki.

'Here is my phone number. Call me if she wants to meet me. If I get what I have come for, I'll pay you more.' Avik put the chit in Sonu's shirt pocket, paid the bill and left.

7

Something had changed within Avik. He could sense it, but could not define it. Surprisingly, he began to dislike the sight of every 'polished' girl that crossed him on his way back to the hotel. He had always been fascinated by the notion of perfect feminine beauty, the parameters of which had been decided long ago by the social guardians. It was only after seeing Ananki that it occurred to him how fake the idea and the norms were.

The perfect skin, the perfect skin colour, the perfect eyebrows, the perfect lips, the perfect nose, the perfect nails, the perfect bust, the perfect waistline, the perfect height are all part of an unrealistic dream instilled in the youth by the media and capitalistic companies to keep their businesses going. These concepts have been internalized to such an extent that they are seen as being 'natural' in the social psyche, he ruminated.

For the first time in his life, Avik began to abhor these preconceived notions of feminine beauty. This realization could only have been brought upon him by someone who did not belong to the very consciousness that had given birth to those limited notions of a woman's beauty.

Ananki is exiled to the outskirts and from the periphery she mocks every social construct that society lauds. What I want to know is what is it that she values?

When he returned to his hotel room, he got into his pyjamas and went straight to his bed. He had no appetite for food. All he wanted to do was to write about his first experience with Ananki before even the slightest part of it slipped his memory. Rather than use his laptop, he wanted to write on paper. He wrote her name across the top of a sheet, using her fountain pen. For a moment he felt as if he could write a million words about her, but the thought of the vision he had had in the afternoon intruded and upset him. He wanted to pull Ananki out of the union with Sernanki that he had envisioned in the afternoon. He was able to write only half a page, which agitated him. He kept the pen and paper aside and went out onto the balcony.

Avik was disturbed by his loss of words. It was as if he had been robbed of his only wealth and he was angry at Ananki for depriving him of it. He was intimidated by the grip in which she held his mind; it had grown stronger with each passing night. No doubt he felt attracted to her, but the attraction that had started out of curiosity, his desire to unravel the unknown, was slowly developing into a triangle of like-hate-fear wherein he lost a part of himself to her at each point. One moment he was attracted to her and the next, the thought of her repulsed him. He knew he had to hold on to his self and that he needed to do so quickly, before the last element of his existence was stolen.

He looked up at the night sky, hoping to detach himself from the pragmatic roar of the road that wanted to engulf him. His eyes locked on to the moon, which appeared slightly larger than usual. He had always been fascinated by it; as a child he had thought that the man in the moon was his twin soul, as lonely and sad as he was. In moments of despair, he had often poured his heart out to him, a patient listener to all his life's miseries, a witness to all his joys and disappointments. He closed his eyes and spread his arms to let the full moon soak him in cool moonlight and wipe away all his travails, bringing tranquillity to his mind.

After a while, Avik began to feel relaxed and clearer-headed than before. *I must keep my mind strong, free from any kind of emotional attachment, whether positive or negative*, he thought as he returned to his bed.

But how do I do it? he wondered.

The question filled him with angst and within no time he found himself drowning in it. As he lay there overwhelmed, his phone rang. It was Khyati.

'Hey, listen, I'm sorry if I upset you this morning. I really did not mean to reach Dr Neerja's house before you and start discussing the case. I was only trying to get some information regarding Ananki's madness from Dr Neerja; you know she does not like to talk about it. If you felt bad, I am sorry,' Khyati hardly took a breath till Avik interrupted her.

He had been thinking of calling her and apologizing for his behaviour and would have done it earlier, had he not been so lost in thinking about how to save himself from Ananki.

'Khyati, I am really sorry for venting my anger on you in the morning. No matter how much I try, I can't erase what I said to you, but I want you to believe that I didn't mean to insult or upset you. You know that, don't you?' he said.

'Yes I do, Avik,' she reassured him.

Avik felt a sense of relief. He felt he could now tell Khyati something that had been on his mind and that he knew she might not like.

'Khyati, I respect you for being there for me, but I guess the path in front of me has room for only one pair of feet. I will keep you updated on my progress, but after this I travel alone,' he said and waited for her reaction, knowing his words would hurt her badly.

Khyati remained silent for few moments. She was hurt indeed, but did not want him to know. Humour had always been her refuge to hide the pain in her heart. Once again Avik had chosen to leave her behind and move ahead on his own.

'I hope that won't stop our "beer dates",' she chuckled.

'No, of course not. I hope you are okay with this?' He wanted to hear it from her, even though he knew she was not okay.

'It's fine with me, Avik,' she replied and paused before continuing, 'It's great that you took this decision. But always remember that I'm just a phone call away.'

Their conversation was cut short by the beep of an incoming call on Avik's phone. He told Khyati that he would call her back and answered the call. It was from a property agent whom Sahay had asked to find an apartment for Avik. Avik quickly wrote the address of his new apartment on the back of the sheet he had used to pen his thoughts on Ananki. The apartment was located in Mayur Vihar in East Delhi. Avik messaged a note of thanks to Sahay and then called Khyati back.

'Will you help me shift to my new place without thinking that I am a selfish person for asking?' he asked.

'Of course I'll help you,' she replied.

Avik felt ashamed and small in front of her, but he wanted to move to the new apartment as soon as possible. He was not familiar with East Delhi and being away from Delhi for so long had made him an outsider. So much had changed since he had moved to Mumbai. Asking Khyati for help seemed a better option than navigating the unknown streets of Mayur Vihar on his own, even if it made her think he was selfish.

She was at his hotel within forty-five minutes. They packed his things and Avik checked out.

'Where are we heading to?' Khyati asked him as he drove.

'Oh, sorry, I forgot to show you the address. Here, take it out from my left pocket.' Avik leaned a bit to allow her to pull the piece of paper out.

Khyati felt a little awkward but pulled the paper out of his pocket. After reading the address and giving him directions, she noticed that something was written overleaf. Curious, she turned the page, but Avik was quick to stop her. The only thing she was able to read was the heading at the top, 'Ananki'.

'I didn't mean to pry, Avik,' she defended her intrusion.

'You will be the first person to read anything I write, Khyati, but when the time is right,' he replied with his eyes fixed on the road.

Khyati folded the sheet of paper and placed it in the glove compartment. The more time she spent with him, the more dejected she felt.

'I should leave now,' she said as soon as he was settled in his new apartment.

'No, don't go yet. We'll have dinner first and then you can decide if you want to go,' he said.

Avik ordered pizza. Khyati was silent throughout dinner, eating quickly. She finished in no time and got up to leave. Avik could sense that he had hurt her and cursed himself for it. He understood the reason for his behaviour towards Khyati and was full of remorse.

The closer he got to Ananki's being, the further he pushed Khyati away. He felt sorry for her. As she stood at his door, he went up to her, held her face between his hands and kissed her. He could taste the cherry lip gloss that she had applied, his tongue roving in her mouth, brushing across her teeth countless times as if surprised at their smoothness. He had not kissed anyone like this before. It was raw, almost animal-like, to the point of being cruel to the receiver.

Khyati shivered several times while he kissed her, with joy, with fear, and like a sponge she absorbed his animal instincts till they were both spent and panting for breath. He immediately felt guilty. He felt his knees going numb but went downstairs to see her off. Her parting hug made him feel all the more contrite. As he walked back up the stairs to his apartment, he thought about how foolish he had been. He did not love Khyati—though he sensed that she had a soft corner for him—and he was stuck in a strange alliance with Ananki.

A kiss at such a juncture was uncalled for. I shouldn't have let myself fall into the trap of chaotic impulses, he frowned at himself.

He felt choked inside, not knowing the way out of his situation, but found solace in beer, drinking till he became forgetful of his own existence.

The next morning, when Avik regained consciousness in his new apartment, it felt to him as if a century had passed while he had lain unconscious. Everything appeared to have gained a new light overnight. The sunlight made the apartment glow with a yellow hue.

It did not look as beautiful at night as it does now. I wish I was not alone.

Avik desired company not because he wanted to share the beauty he saw but because he feared loneliness. He thought of Ananki. No matter how hard he tried to resist her, he could not, as if she were inevitable. He wanted to treat her as just another source of information important for the story, but something pushed him beyond that boundary.

For me she stands true to her name, he thought as he headed towards the kitchen.

Ananki recognized the scarf that Avik had tied to one of the bars of the door to her cell, which prompted her to ask Dr Neerja if her sister had visited her, though in her own style of communication. Her eyes filled with tears as she wrote 'Priyanka?' on the wall, large enough for the doctor to read it.

None of her family members had visited her before. As she returned to stand in front of Dr Neerja, the doctor shook her head. She then took the scarf from Ananki's hand and tied it around the young girl's neck, but Ananki, clearly upset, pulled it off and threw it away from herself.

'Da?' she whispered.

It was the first word she had spoken since she had entered her cell.

Stunned, Dr Neerja turned around. 'Who?' she asked.

'Da came here to see me?' Ananki asked in a low voice, as if she had said something forbidden, clutching the bars with both hands out of anxiety.

'I am afraid it was not Da. But you did have a visitor after all this time, a young man. He met Priyanka, and she gave him some of your belongings. I made it clear to him that you don't want to meet anyone from the outside world. That's what I have been instructed by Mr Rajput as well.'

Dr Neerja waited for a response from Ananki, then left the cell for a meeting with Mr Rajput regarding Avik's visit.

On seeing Dr Neerja going out of the NGO, Sonu went to Ananki's cell and gave her the mouth organ. She picked it up from the floor. She could not believe she was holding a gift most precious to her. She closed her eyes and felt the touch of its body on her palms.

As Sonu turned to leave, Ananki stopped him.

'Who gave it to you? Da?' she asked.

'No madam, Avik sir asked me to give it you. He came to see you yesterday and wanted to meet you again, but Dr Neerja didn't allow him,' he replied.

'Did he tell you why he wanted to meet me?' Ananki's tone showed signs of inquisitiveness.

'No madam, but he gave me five thousand rupees just to help him reach out to you. It must be of some importance,' he said.

Sonu's revelation made Ananki more curious.

'Can you bring him here?' she asked him.

'We will have to wait till the next opportunity,' he told Ananki and left.

8

Avik's head was heavy and his nerves begged for tea, but there was no milk or sugar in the kitchen. The previous tenant, however, had left some tea in a small container. He made black tea and forced it down as he went in search of his mobile.

There were nine missed calls and three messages. One was from Sahay, asking about the new apartment and the progress on the case. Khyati had messaged him to call her when he woke up, signing off with a heart. He felt as if he had landed himself in trouble again, after the indifferent break-up with Trisha. The third message was from Sonu, received only forty-five minutes ago, asking Avik to call back. He had also called him thrice. Avik called Sonu back, ignoring the other two. He answered the phone in a tone more cheerful than the last meeting.

'Avik sir, I gave Ananki madam the mouth organ. She said she wants to meet the person who sent it to her,' Sonu said.

Avik felt his body relaxing because of the words he had just heard.

'Did she say anything else?' he asked.

'At first she thought it was someone else who had sent the mouth organ. She was not taking any name but said something strange.' Sonu paused for a while.

'What was it?' Avik was anxious to know.

'Something like, "Da",' Sonu replied.

Avik remembered how she had also addressed the letter to this person.

'So when can I meet her?' Avik came back to the point. 'Luck is in your favour, Avik sir. Dr Neerja is going out of Delhi for four days. You come tomorrow at 1 p.m., lunchtime. It is the safest,' Sonu replied excitedly, thinking about the money he would get from Avik.

In her office, Dr Neerja kept thinking about Ananki and Avik. She wondered what had made Ananki break her long silence and be curious about a boy she knew nothing of. Was it because Avik had made an effort to probe into her life, proof of which was the scarf, the sight of which had prompted her to inquire about him?

But Avik's interest in Ananki appears greater than that of a journalist's in an important witness. He is delving more and more deeply into this case, to the point of developing a strong infatuation for the girl, if I have observed correctly. Even Mr Rajput has been reminding me not to let Ananki meet anyone and he sounded quite stern in the meeting when I updated him regarding Avik. If Avik persists any further, I will have to ask Mr Rajput to take action.

Avik had had an intuition that he would meet Ananki, but he had not expected it to happen so soon. A fleeting feeling of calm possessed him until he realized that the fated event was to take place the following day and he was not prepared at all. He had never met someone who had been in a mental institution. The thought gave him goosebumps, his limbs turned cold while a sweat broke out on his forehead. He had watched her covertly, but meeting her face-to-face would be a challenge. He kept wondering what was it that had made her curious enough to meet him.

Is there some trickery on her mind? Is it even safe to meet her?

He could not understand why he was so hesitant to meet her. *It was I who tied the scarf to the door of her cell, hoping she would notice that I had been there. It was I who gave the mouth organ to Sonu to give to her so that she might want to meet me. It is all going according to my plan, but something is pulling me back.*

He felt on guard, his mind warning him of what lay ahead, but a small part of his self knew no restrictions. It was like a tiny feather that could not be caught – the more Avik tried to hold on to it, the further it drifted away from him. What bothered him was that it was drifting towards her.

The next morning arrived in the blink of an eye.

Someone must have bribed Time to speed up its wheel, he complained as he silenced the alarm clock.

No matter how hard he tried to hurry, he felt himself running short of time. It was already 10 in the morning and he had neither had a shower nor eaten breakfast.

'I must not be late at any cost,' he muttered as he went to the bathroom.

After shaving off his beard, which had grown significantly as he had not shaved in several days, he went to the cupboard to select the clothes he was going to wear. He picked a white shirt, not caring how dirty it might get. His strong deodorant was rejected in favour of subtle cologne. All his efforts were directed at making himself as inconspicuous as possible.

Today is not the day to project myself onto her, but to make her project herself onto me in every way she can.

He put all her belongings in his bag and left his apartment without eating any breakfast. He had been eating very little since he had taken up this case. He did not feel hunger, as he was preoccupied with Ananki all the time.

As he neared the institution, he was filled with a fearful uneasiness. He parked the car but forgot to lock it, mindlessly picking up the bag that contained Ananki's belongings.

She is about to unlock her closet while I am about to lock myself within, he contemplated as he entered the building.

He felt he was no longer the same man as he walked down the corridor. Avik waited for Sonu in the corridor itself. Lost in his own thoughts, he didn't see him coming. Avik remained unaware of his presence until he felt the touch of his hand on Sonu's shoulder.

He quivered as if someone had pinched him out of a nightmare. Sonu handed him a tissue, but he did not understand what he should use it for till he felt the sweat trickling down his forehead. He took it, wiped his brow, then stood up to go meet Ananki. Seeing his state, Sonu got a bit worried. He handed him a glass of water.

Avik drank the water and assured Sonu that he was just a little nervous, but Sonu noticed that something more troubled him.

'Are you sure you are ready to meet her?' Sonu asked.

'Yes. I am fine. Really. It's just that I haven't been in a situation like this before. I don't know what to say when I meet her and it's making me jittery,' Avik said as they walked towards the stairs leading to the basement.

'I would advise you not to say much. Just let her do the talking. Be a patient listener, that is what Dr Neerja does all the time with patients like her,' Sonu said, trying to calm him.

He patted Avik's back twice and then left him at the stairs, all by himself.

The light on the staircase was as dim as before. Avik walked down carefully, to avoid making any sound. He heard the faint sound of music, which grew louder at each step. As he reached the bottom of the staircase, he realized that it was a tune being played on the mouth organ. It was her. His feet turned cold, as if the blood had frozen inside them, as if the music had paralysed him. He sat on the last step to prevent himself from falling.

The upper part of his body was sweating heavily while below his waist he was frigid. He felt that if he took even a step further, his body would break into two. He removed his shoes and started to rub his feet to thaw them. The music echoed in the space surrounding him. It called out to him. He put his cold feet back into his shoes, stood up and walked towards its source. He reached the door of Ananki's cell.

There she was, lying on her back, her hair left loose and spread out behind her, covering nearly the entire room. He sat down facing the cell without making any sound.

Her hands are holding the mouth organ I once held. Her lips are touching it where I once pressed my lips. Blowing softly into the instrument, she makes the most beautiful music I have ever heard, Avik mused as he looked at her, not wanting her to stop playing.

He watched her play, unaware of how long he did so, until he felt something brush his shoulder. He shrugged it off and stood up in a flurry, wondering how someone could survive in such a creepy place.

She must be mad to want to stay in a place like this when she can move to the women's ward. Only a beast would like to live here amongst other beasts, he thought in anger.

The music stopped. The stir had made 'the beast' aware of being watched. He saw that she had turned to face the opposite wall. He did not know if she had stopped because she had seen him or because of the sound he had made.

Who could see anyone in such a dark dungeon?

But while he was accustomed to the brightness of the world above, her eyes were capable of seeing through the darkness between them. In the grey darkness one can see those things that hide themselves in the presence of light. Black might appear grey in the presence of white, but in grey, black appears in its real hue.

He stood there holding the bars, then saw the scarf lying on the floor nearby. He picked it up and tied it around his neck, clearing his throat to attract her attention. She did not turn around but saw his reflection in the silver of the mouth organ, and then hurled it at him. It sailed through the bars and hit his chest, making him groan. He kept his right hand on his chest where he had been struck and leant against the closed wooden door of the room opposite her cell. He wished he could open the door to her cell and grab her by her hair, pulling the insanity out of her.

Pain can indeed turn a human into a monster. Her aggression was no doubt the result of a torment she had borne in the past. She was venting her anger out on him for trying to infiltrate her space. It appeared that she had called Avik in order to punish him for the other day. He had dared to gaze upon her without her consent and she was penalizing him for it.

She giggled, making him all the more upset. He pulled the scarf from around his neck and threw it into her cell. She leapt up and caught it before it could touch the ground, then draped it across her shoulders before coming to stand close to the bars.

There was a challenge in the way she looked at him. He was not a man to let a woman's challenge go unanswered. With unblinking eyes he held out the mouth organ. Her hand immediately reached out to grab it.

The bars that stood between them clanked suddenly, startling them. Her food had arrived. Avik stood back as Sonu unlocked the door. Ananki pulled herself back till she hit the wall opposite the bars, showing no interest in the food. The tray was placed on the floor and the door was locked again. Sonu whispered to Avik to follow him. Avik nodded, but there was something he wished to tell Ananki before he left.

'By what you did today, you proved wrong one of the two people who thought you were not mad. I think it is fair to keep you caged in a place like this, for that's what you deserve. I was foolish to think that I could help you. The truth is, no one can help you. No one will ever come to help you after today,' so saying, Avik left like a bullet released from its chamber, making up his mind never to see her again.

He could have borne her aggressive gaze, her tormenting music, even her stinging words, but physical assault was too much for him.

Avik was still upset and made it clear to himself that he had done whatever he could for Ananki and that this was the end of it. The fact that he would not be able to print her story was already a blow to his dream, but being assaulted by a madwoman on top of that was too much. It had deeply offended his ego.

Avik spent the entire night trying to convince himself that he could erase Ananki from his consciousness forever. Dawn came with the cognizance that the only thought that had been in his mind since he had returned from the institution was of her. *Attraction or repulsion, liking or hatred are the dualities of emotions she invokes in me. Any one of them is constantly present in my mind. There is never a moment of indifference.*

I cannot kill her ever. I must go back to her, not for the story's sake, not for her own sake, but for myself, he thought.

Avik called Sonu to ask if he could meet Ananki one more time.

When he arrived at the NGO, he was taken down to her cell immediately. He stood outside it quietly. She saw him and got to her feet. She went to the wall and flipped a switch, allowing light to illuminate the dungeon. It not only surprised Avik but also made him conscious of her gaze. Her big black eyes examined him from top to bottom as she moved towards him.

In order to avoid eye contact with her he fixed his eyes on the mouth organ, which lay in exactly the same spot as it had been in the previous day, till she stood before him, obstructing his view. He feared another assault from her and went pale, not knowing what to do. She bent her knees a little to intersect the line of his vision, her lips curving a little to break into a smile as she met his eyes, making him feel more and more vulnerable.

He reached inside his bag and took out the book of sonnets. The smile vanished suddenly and she stepped back. He opened the book to the page that had been marked by a folded corner. He looked at her once before starting to recite Sonnet 142. A thrill went through him as he recited the second-last line to her, 'If thou dost seek to have what thou dost hide…' but she snatched the book from his hands before he could read the last line. She pulled the page from the book and tore it to pieces. He saw tears brimming in her deep eyes, eyes that could hold an ocean.

'How dare you? Get out of here and never come back, you thief. Get lost!' she howled like a mad wolf and spit on him.

This was the second time his ego had received a jolt from her. It made him very angry. He clenched his fists tightly and banged them on the bars, only to hurt himself. He felt his hands going numb with pain. He spit back, not on her but on the ground, and left the basement. In his anger he appeared to be her twin soul, just as mad as her; only he did not realize it.

She was the creator of her self-inflicted madness, which she used as a shield, but he, like any other individual, created madness within himself without being aware of it.

Her mask of madness kept out the prying eyes that made her suffer by labelling her. Any deviation from the social norm was madness. So be it. For her there was no harm in being labelled as mad if it kept her safe. Only madness would let her remain what she wanted to be and act the way she desired. Unlike him, the only force that governed her actions was the one inside her and it made her push him away in fright at one moment and pull him towards her the very next. He had tried to puncture her mask and it gave him an autonomy that she feared.

By the time Avik reached his apartment, he had decided that it was time for him to return to Mumbai. As he was packing his bags, Sonu arrived with an envelope. He took it without much interest, kept it on his desk and continued to fold his clothes. Worn out both physically and mentally, he slept soon after he finished packing, completely forgetting about the envelope.

While getting ready to leave for the airport the next morning, his eye fell on the white envelope lying on the desk. He opened it to find a half-dried leaf from the book of sonnets. He read the three words written on it with charcoal, 'One Last Time', followed by her name.

He found it hard to believe that Ananki had written to him. Her handwriting was bewitching and, just like before, he felt it try to pull him inside the leaf.

This time, however, he insisted on staying grounded in reality and going back to Mumbai. The cab had arrived. On the way to the airport he took the leaf out of his pocket numerous times, reading it and putting it back, as if he had become akin to Sisyphus. But while Sisyphus had had no way of escaping his futile existence, Avik found his path. He told the driver to take him to Dr Neerja's NGO. He took the recorder out of his bag and put it in his pocket, hoping that it would prove to be useful this time.

Sonu was waiting for him in the corridor. He accompanied Avik to Ananki's cell. Halting by the stairs to keep a watch, he asked Avik to keep the meeting as short as possible.

Avik saw Ananki standing at the bars, waiting for him. She pressed her lips together as he came near her, as if giving him a secret smile, and then asked for her diary. He pulled it out at once and handed it to her. She opened the combination lock and sat down beside the bars. He could not believe that he was the one chosen to witness and be part of her tale. He sat down opposite her.

'I will read excerpts from my diary, things that I wrote long ago in order to free myself from despair. But I will do so on one condition,' Ananki said and waited for his affirmation. When he nodded, she continued, 'You will not interrupt or question me. If you do, I will stop there and then.'

'Okay.' Avik had no choice but to agree.

9

Being made to sleep alone as a child just because one wets the bed—something one has no control over—can make anyone feel abandoned. I had been sleeping alone ever since I could remember. Radha, the caretaker my parents had hired for me, told me that I had been sleeping in a separate room since I was two years old. Wasn't I too young for my parents to dump me to sleep in a huge bed all by myself, while they had their share of privacy? They never knew how I felt, not even my mother. Several times I would tie myself to her with the end of her saree so that I could sleep with her, on their bed, but their fear of their bed getting spoilt never allowed me my share of security as a child. At night the expensive toys that my parents bought to be my companions would change their shapes and become something else. They would perform a strange dance, floating over my head as I tried to sleep. When I would close my eyes I felt as if they would pick me up and throw me into the wide sewer just opposite our bungalow. For hours I would open and shut my eyes to find out what was real, the bed or the sewer, until I fell asleep. They scared me even in my dreams, tormenting me with thousands of pricks on my skin; that is when I would release the water, to stop them. They were scared of getting wet, I guess. I had developed it as a defence mechanism, much to the dismay of my parents.

Once, I had this dream in which I was playing in the park where Radha would take me every evening. After playing for a while I felt really hot. I asked her for water, but she would not give it to me. When I yelled at her, she told me that Mom had told her not to give me any water when I felt hot. I felt my insides burn. I was shouting and crying for water. I asked the people who were in the park with their kids for water, but no one came to help me. The heat inside my body was rising rapidly. My body temperature increased so much that my hair caught fire. I did not know what to do. I kept running like a mad dog but could not extinguish the fire in my hair. My head was burning and there was no water to save me. So I had to release it to save myself.

When I was six years old, my parents planned a summer camping expedition. I was very excited about the fact that I would be spending a lot of time with my family. During the day we went boating. I rushed towards the red boat and sat in my father's lap but Mom asked me to go sit in the blue boat with Radha. She said that only two people could sit in one boat. I was sad but I obeyed, thinking we would have a good time later in our tent. But Mom and Dad stayed in one tent and Radha and I had to stay in another. Radha did not even let me go to the campfire, saying that it was time for kids to sleep. I was not feeling sleepy. I wanted to go out and talk to my parents, but I was forced to lie in my bed and keep my eyes shut. I pretended to have fallen asleep. Seeing me asleep, Radha turned off the lamp and went to sleep on the mattress next to mine. When I could hear her snores, I opened the entrance flap of the tent and saw the campfire. It was glowing with yellow flames. Beside it were Mom and Dad, wrapped in each other's arms under one blanket. He kissed her with a passion greater than that of the fire burning beside them. He lifted her up and took her to their tent, switching off the lamp while going in. I got the chance to go and sit beside the campfire. I kept staring at the fire, not realizing when it turned from yellow to red. Just then a huge lizard came towards me. It was big, like a snake. I passed water so that it would not come near me. It did not. But it stuck its long tongue out and licked my heel, maybe thinking it to be a grasshopper. Radha woke me up to change my clothes and the bed sheet.

For seven years I had to cope with the loneliness. I got the news of the arrival of another baby in the house. I was so happy, thinking how great that would be. I would have a companion. I dreamt of playing with the baby all day. I wanted to take care of it, feed it, change its diapers, tell it bedtime stories and snuggle in bed with it till we both lost ourselves to sleep. I would not have to suffer the torment of sleeping alone. I was happy inside my heart. But nothing of that sort happened. The baby had to sleep with its mother. I saw the baby being breastfed by my mother. I could not remember if I had ever been fed by her. All I remembered was the plastic bottle and the succulent rubber nipple that had fed me for four long years. I remembered how I *used to chew on it out of fear and rage, widening its hole, and then it would pour out an enormous amount of milk in my mouth, making me regurgitate it. It had to be replaced almost every week. But the baby was never given the rubber nipple. I asked Radha why it was not fed with the bottle. She told me that only a mother's milk can make one strong. So the seven-year-old in me concluded that I had been rendered weak right from my birth.*

Being a weakling can play havoc with one's mind. My mind was as violent as a hurricane, only my dear ones could not feel it. I would batter my teddies and dolls, spoil their faces with ink. One day I broke the neck of my Barbie. I hated them all. No matter how much I tried, they could not fill up my empty childhood. While I suffered, the new baby got all of my parents' attention. My mother stopped going away as she used to each morning. She stayed at home with the new baby. Everyone said that I had had a sister. My mother would keep her in her lap for hours. I remembered that when I had wanted to sit in her lap she would tell me that she was too tired. Sometimes on my father's insistence she would let me place my head on her lap, but soon she would ask me to remove it. She would tell me that she was not strong enough to hold me for a long time. I wondered from where she had gained her new-found strength. My heart cried on seeing the two of them hug the baby a thousand times a day and never tire of it. The baby would receive a hundred kisses while I craved just one. I was the ugly, rejected child, cared for by no one, remembered by no one and loved by no one.

Lack of love and attention from my parents killed my appetite, making me lean as a stick. The ugliness of my frame made me even more repulsive to my mother. She would not look at me for several days together. She thought she had done her duty by hiring a caretaker for me. In the lone hours of my desperation I would question the kind of parenting given to me and compare it with that bestowed upon my sister. When I needed them, my parents' priority was their job and business respectively. They both wanted to make it big. They earned a lot of money and fame, but at the cost of my innocent childhood.

Almost every night, I went to sleep crying on my pillow. My eyes would be swollen in the morning, but no one had the time to notice. Sometimes Dad would ask me if I had overslept, if that was why my eyes were swollen. How could he know what I was going through when he was away from home most of the time? I used to think that if he spent more time with us, then he would at least try to understand me, but god did not want my miseries to be any less.

My attention span at school was poor. My mind was always preoccupied with the emotional trauma I was suffering at home. I hardly learnt anything in any of my classes. My classwork was always incomplete. No one at home ever reviewed my homework. I was thrashed every day by my teacher, who made me stand with my hands raised as punishment. One after another every one of my teachers would punish me, without trying to learn what my real problem was. Neither did my parents try to understand me. They didn't have the time. They had a very busy life. My interest in studies and school deteriorated with time. My mother already had innumerable reasons to be upset with me, and my poor academic performance added fuel to her anger. I could never *tell what distressed her more, the fact that I did not do well in school or the embarrassment she faced every time she had to visit my school for a parent-teacher meeting.*

I craved love, both giving and receiving it. I felt that the enormous amount of love pent up inside me would explode one day and I would waste it all. I had a tremendous need to share the love within me, but there was no one on whom I could shower it. One day I saw my baby sister lying on the bed in my parents' room, playing with her rattle, while Mom had gone for a bath. She was wearing a pink floral-print dress. Her white hands moved briskly, making the rattle produce a musical sound. Each sound was followed by her giggle, as if she was pleased by her newly acquired skill. The sight tempted me to enter the room and sit beside her. But soon she lost interest in the rattle and starting crying. I tried to pat her so that she would know she wasn't alone, but she did not stop. I kissed her and held her hand, gave her my index finger to hold and play with, but nothing worked. I had often seen Mom carrying and rocking her to soothe her when she was crying loudly. I thought that was the only way she would stop crying. I lifted her in my arms. It was the first time that I was holding anything other than a non-living entity. I held her close to myself for a few seconds, felt her warmth, but she would not quiet down. I tried to rock her to soothe her, but I was still a child myself. She slipped out of my hands and fell onto the bed, making her cry even harder than before. I was petrified. Out of fear of Mom's scolding I put a blanket over my sister so that her shrill cries would not be heard. But the blanket was ineffective. Hearing the loud cries, my mother immediately came out of the bathroom, wearing her bathrobe. She quickly removed the blanket covering my sister and picked her up. She rubbed her back, but it did not help. She called Radha to take me away.

After a few minutes my sister's cries subsided. Mom was really angry and she came up to my room. In all these years, she had hardly ever entered my room; she always said that she could not bear the stench of urine. She entered that day only to beat me black and blue. Slippers, shoes, ruler, broom, she beat me with everything that she could lay her hands on. For nearly ten minutes I could feel the blows on my body. According to her it was a befitting punishment for my action. I couldn't understand which action she was referring to, that I wanted to love my sister or that I had accidentally dropped her on the bed.

I had loved my sister for one minute and received a beating for ten minutes. That was my fate. I had heard many elders say that to be worthy of love, one should first give love. I gave love and got thrashed in return. I kept asking myself if love was so hard to get.

My mother narrated the incident to my father over the phone and he wished to speak to me about it. I was summoned from my room. As I walked to the phone, I kept thinking about what he would say to me. Would he also scold me or would he listen to me? What if he never wished to speak to me again? The thought made me shudder. As my hand reached for the receiver, I realized that I was weeping, not because I had been beaten but for the fear of losing his love. On hearing me sob, he asked me to tell him what had happened, though I was sure he already knew. It made me feel better. I promised him that I did not intend to hurt my sister and that I would never do it again.

The following week he gifted me a pup. My joy knew no bounds. When all others failed to understand my basic need for love, he saw through me and gave me a sweetheart to hold and kiss whenever I wanted. I called my puppy Ray, as he had brought hope into my bleak life; hope to give love and this time to receive love as well.

Ray was a real companion at home. As soon as I returned from school and entered the main gate, he would rush out to lick my feet in adoration. He would accompany me to my room. Wait for me as I changed my clothes. His food and water bowls were kept in my room. My mother did not want him to make the entire home untidy. I used to leave him out in the garden so he could ease himself. I never chained him. He was a smart dog and returned after emptying his bowels on his own. In the evening I would run around in our garden and he would chase me. He was a true friend, the only friend I made in my life. Day after day my love for him increased, but my mother's tolerance was inversely proportional to my love. One day she asked our gatekeeper to blindfold Ray and leave him somewhere far away so that he would not come back. She could no longer see my dog disturbing the sanctity of her home. She told my father that the dog was unhygienic and harmful for the baby. He could not argue; after all, he did not wish any harm to come to the baby either. Ray left me. Love left me too.

One day Radha forgot to place a clean towel in my bathroom. After taking a shower I stood in front of the mirror, naked, to dry off the excess water from my skin. I noticed that my body had developed fatty areas on my chest. I was confused, as I was skinny otherwise. How could they grow overnight? Or had I not paid attention to my body before that day? I stood there looking at myself. Suddenly someone knocked on the door. I went to the door and peeked out. It was Radha. She had brought me my towel. I noticed that she too had the same fatty areas. As I thought about it, I realized that so did Mom and my teacher. It seemed every woman had them. Was I also becoming a woman? The sight of myself in the mirror pleased me. But then there was something else that appalled me, the dark hair under my armpits. I had seen Mom wearing sleeveless dresses. She was so clean and beautiful while I had these ugly black curls that shamed me. Not only in the areas visible just to me but also above my lips. I had thick eyebrows and side locks that made me look grotesque. I felt like crying. I cursed God for making me like that.

My school prayers taught us that every single person is God's own creation. If I was also made by His hand, why was I not considered beautiful? There was madness around me for a certain idea of beauty. I could never be a part of that madness. I remained an outsider forever. My sister was an angel. A healthy and happy child. She was showered with everyone's love. She was perfect, according to my parents, a daughter they could boast of, in beauty and manners.

When Priyanka was five, my mother decided to teach her how to swim. I saw them in the swimming pool. Mom was holding her by her waist while she moved her hands and legs to and fro; it was as if a little tadpole was swimming with its mother. That day I realized the extent of the lack of a mother's love in my life. I went to the edge of the swimming pool and called out to my mother. She looked at me and asked me to wait. I shouted that I too wanted to learn. She told me that since I was bigger now, she would not be able to bear my weight in the water. She told me that she would send me to a professional instructor if I wanted to learn. I had always been given into the hands of others by my parents. My childhood had been lost to their business. Now that they were millionaires, they could spare time for Priyanka. But how could I rewind my clock? How could I get my childhood back to relive it the way I had always wanted it to be? I could not and neither could their money. I felt doomed. Just then an idea struck me. I thought that if I could end my life and be born again as a baby, I could gain back those lost years. Radha had once told me that people who die are born again. There is something within us that never ends. That something comes back when the body is gone.

I stepped into the pool, going down the steps one by one, the water rising higher and higher with each step. I could feel it at my throat. I stopped to think that if this was the last time I was alive, who would miss my presence. Would my mother miss me after my death? I did not think so. My sister was too young to even notice my presence. Radha might be upset by my untimely death, as it would mean the loss of her job. My death would bring sadness to only one person in this house: Dad. The thought was more suffocating than the water around me. But then he had his work, Mom and Priyanka to cheer him up. I held the least priority in his life too. After mourning me for some days, he would be back to going on his business trips and the memory of me would fade away in no time. When my living presence did not cross his mind when he was away from *home then how could the memory of me trouble him when I was gone? He would be fine too eventually.*

I closed my eyes and bent my knees. I could feel the water gushing into me through my nose, mouth and ears. I felt as if the entire swimming pool was floating in my head. After that I ceased to feel anything till I woke up in my father's arms. He had saved me from drowning. He looked worried and held me for a long time. That was the first time I remember being hugged by him.

'Don't you ever do anything stupid like that ever again. Your life belongs not only to you but also to the people who love you. You have no right to take it away. We all love you. You don't want us to feel cheated, do you?'

I felt loved and cared for. Some of my assumptions had been proved wrong. I mended the neck of the Barbie he had bought for me when I was seven. I ate well and kept myself tidy. Soon my health and physique improved. The curls on my head grew till my waist. I let Radha braid them for school so I would look neat. I started to take care of myself, not for my sake but to gain his affection. He began to work from home most of the time while my mother went to her office. I stopped going out to play so that I could spend more time watching him work, doing my homework by his side.

When Mom was travelling for work, Radha would take care of Priyanka while I was left on my own.

Once in her absence I had to braid my hair myself. No matter how much I tried I could not do it. My hair was not in my control. Even Mom could not handle it. Only Radha could manage my curls. I went to my father's home office to fetch a pair of scissors. I opened the drawer of his desk and took out the scissors without his permission while he watched. I held the scissors in one hand and my hair in the other and was about to cut it when he shouted out to me from the couch. He rushed towards me and took the scissors from my hand. I started crying in desperation. He picked me up and took me to my room, made me sit on his lap and oiled my hair, braiding it beautifully. How pretty I looked. For a child like me who had never received even a glimmer of attention from anyone, his caring help, however little it was, sowed the seed of a deep-rooted affection in my heart.

Ever since I could remember, I was indifferent to people, detached from everyone, not only because everyone was too occupied with their lives but also because no one cared to make any effort with me either. A child only needs its parents' time and love, nothing else. No matter how much wealth my parents accumulated, no matter how many toys they bought me, no matter how reputed an international school they sent me to, it all came to naught in my eyes. A child's worst fear is loneliness, but not just a child's—it can kill the most powerful of creatures. I felt as if the loneliness within me had developed jaws that sucked my marrow more with each passing day. These jaws fed upon me and grew stronger. My father was the only one who tried to save me from being sucked into those jaws completely. It was he who erased my indifference by his acts of caring. But he never showed his affection in the presence of my mother. He loved my mother a lot and listened to every word that she said as a command. She did not like to spend anything on me, be it her time or money; only she never said so openly.

I was about to enter my teens. It is the age when parents play the most crucial role in one's life—that of a guide. Just as Lord Krishna gave the knowledge of the Bhagvada Gita to his disciple and friend Arjuna to prevent him from straying from the right path, such is the parents' duty towards their teenage child. The right guidance by parents can encourage a child to make the right choices at the right time, but the lack of such guidance can lead to lifelong repentance.

I was good at literature. In fact, I thrived on it, Shakespeare in particular. It soothed my tormented senses. I wanted to become a poet, for I was gifted with imagination, although I lacked proficiency in language. I wanted to join a language class so that I could paint my imagination in words that would not fail me. But the age of poetry had died long ago, according to my mother. The world of my imagination waited for the right words and direction, but just like Godot, they never came. I felt like I was sailing in an endless sea of my imagination, not knowing in which direction to sail, not knowing where the shore of language might be. And so poetry perished.

Asking for artistic guidance from my parents might have been too much for them, as their life was based on finance. But asking for physiological guidance from a mother is never too much. My mother never cared to notice my maturing physical self. I learnt about the things that a mother should explain to her daughter from various other sources such as classmates, magazines and television. I remember the day I got my period for the first time, soiling my white uniform. Everyone in my class saw the stain, but I did not know the reason for their stares. The boys giggled, the girls were shocked, but no one approached me to help. My stomach hurt like hell. I thought I should pass urine to ease the pain. I saw blood. I could not understand what had happened. I had not fallen or gotten hurt, so why was I bleeding? I started crying and would not come out of the school lavatory. Finally, one of my classmates told my teacher that I had not returned from the girls' toilet. My teacher sent her to check on me. I feared I would die from the continuous bleeding from my insides. I told her what was happening to me, to which she replied that it was normal and happened to all females.

She knew about it, I did not. She was prepared for it, while I was taken aback, totally unprepared. She took me to the school clinic where I was given a sanitary napkin and a skirt to change into. My classmate taught me how to use the pad, disconcerted at my lack of knowledge. I didn't tell my mother about my period for a long time.

It was because of my mother's apathy and my father's uxorious nature that my birthday had never been celebrated; at least, I don't remember it. It was only on my fourteenth birthday when she was away on a business trip that my father decided to celebrate it. He asked me to invite all my friends. He was surprised to find that I did not invite anyone from my school or the neighbourhood. I had no friends to share this moment of my life. Radha had prepared my favourite dishes. Dad brought a cake for me in the evening. It was a replica of our home. He gifted me my home as my birthday present. He sang the birthday song and handed me a knife while I blew out the candles. I looked at the cake. After fourteen years of my life my father had given my home to me. How could I cut it?

Tears trickled down my cheeks, leaving him stunned. He came and stood next to me and whispered in my ear, 'Just close your eyes and capture this moment in your memory, and then it will stay there forever.'

He wiped away my tears and made me smile. I looked at the cake-that-was-home, then turned my gaze to him and closed my eyes. I wished for many more returns of this moment and cut my birthday cake. It became my best memory with him.

Memories have always been very important to me. For it was Dad who told me about the power that resides in memories. They turn everything immortal, showering permanence on otherwise fleeting moments. I kept saving memories of love and kindness whenever I could find them. I had become a memory gatherer, to the extent that I lived not only in my memories but in the hope of adding more memories to my existing cache.

Everyone has their special moments in life, everyone remembers them. But simply remembering them was not what I did. I relived them in my mind, in empty moments of desperation and pain when I had no one around; I started performing memories from my cache to fill the vacuum in my spirit, as if the theatre in my mind staged the show of my life. Were the characters real? I did not know. I lived in two worlds, the empty pragmatic world that gave me nothing but affliction, and the one in my mind, the world of infinite bliss. Day after day as my store of memories filled the void, I began to immerse myself more and more in the world of my memories. I would spend hours in my room, living within the play of my memories.

Radha noticed that I would stay locked inside my room for long periods of time and started to worry about me. She thought that I talked to myself more than I should. Once I tried to explain to her that I didn't talk to myself but to them. She did not believe me. Instead, she told my father what I had said, and he became really worried. He came to see me every evening and asked me the same questions over and over again. 'Who do you talk to?' I told him that I was able to spend time with Ray despite his absence, I told him that I spent time with him too, but he did not believe me, telling me that the things I spoke about had never happened. He thought it best to take me to a doctor who asked me strange questions, after which he jumped to the conclusion that I spoke to imaginary people because my mind was cheating on me.

But the people I saw were not imaginary; they were the real people from my life, my best friend Ray and my father. All I did was enact some of the memories I had of them. I confess that some events I did invent, but only things that I wished would happen in my life, nothing else. I never saw or imagined any random person. But the doctor thought otherwise. He asked my father to keep a watch on me and prescribed some medication too.

Dad gave strict instructions to Radha to monitor my medication and my mind's plays. Everyone was after me to wipe out this imaginary world of mine. But this world in my mind was the real world for me. It was the source of my existence. My happiness was secured in this personal space, which was now being intruded upon by my own people. It was time to lock the door and throw away the key. The stage shifted; the action and dialogues became internal. According to them I was getting better. Radha no longer heard me talking to myself. She saw me sitting on my bed most of the time, or in my rocking chair, eyes closed. No one realized that a storm was approaching. Not even me.

As I grew up, I realized that God's best creation was not the human being but the human mind. And not just any mind, but a mind that could feel and relive the memories that it stored. Memories that could bring back lost happiness and complete an otherwise incomplete life. I gained another level of understanding about the power of memories. Not all memories please one; some are there to haunt one for the rest of one's life. I was fifteen years old when I encountered one such memory that not only tormented me but also changed the course of my existence.

It was the night when a part of me died forever, while a part of me blossomed in a new light.

My parents were hosting a terrace party. Mom had always been the perfect hostess. My parents enjoyed collecting rare artefacts. But my mother differed from my father in one aspect: not only was she fond of buying rarities but also of showing them off. And whenever they made a new acquisition, she would throw a party to let the world know what a great eye she had been born with.

Most of the guests had arrived. My parents were busy attending to them. At least I thought so. I never liked these gatherings. Being around too many people suffocated me. I did not want to join the party and told Radha that I was not feeling well. She told me to go to bed and went to get my medicine. Half an hour passed but she did not return. I left my room to get the medicine myself. The medicine box was not in its usual *place in the den. I thought Mom must have taken it to her room and forgotten to put it back. I went to my parents' bedroom barefoot. I was scared, for if she saw me like that, she would scold me.*

The door was open. I peeped inside the room. It was all clear. I tiptoed to Mom's desk and started searching for the box. It was not in the first drawer. I opened the second one without making the slightest noise. A sound startled me. It came from the bathroom attached to my parents' bedroom. I went to the closed door of the bathroom and pressed my ear against it. Someone was in there. But my parents were upstairs. I thought a thief had broken in. I clutched the doorknob tightly and slowly opened the door. I peeked in. There, in the shower stall, stood a man covered in white foam from head to toe. He was tall and looked like a snowman, only a little leaner. He was the first naked man I had ever seen. His was the first frame I had ever known. Every single part of him looked desirable. The sight mesmerized me. I felt no guilt in looking at his naked body as he rubbed his nether parts. It was a moment of glory. But then every moment of glory is packed within a bubble that must burst as soon as it shows itself. While I stood captivated, staring unblinking at him, he turned on the shower, and as he turned his face towards the door my sanity was washed away with the foam. He was my father.

I saw what I should not have seen. The burden of that moment's guilt was to be carried all my life. I closed the door and tiptoed back to my room, locking it from the inside. I threw myself face down on my bed, burying my face in my pillow. I felt like crying out loud, but my eyes did not release even a single tear. Had I cried that night I would have felt better. I might have gotten rid of it. But nothing of the sort happened. I did not cry. Instead, the sight of him kept obstructing my vision. When I closed my eyes I saw him again. I could not sleep. His image was imprinted on my mind. Ugly thoughts started to creep in. I wanted to shoo them away but they would not leave. I wished I could slice off the part of my mind from where his image kept springing up, torturing me, mocking me in every way possible. It spread within my mind like a contagious disease, leaving none of my faculties in their right form.

The vision of him engulfed my mind completely. I could think of nothing else, see nothing else, desire nothing else. It travelled within me from top to bottom, from my mind, to my heart and then to my nether parts. I fell in love with my own father, but not the way daughters love their dads. He assumed a dual role in my life, that of Da-d and also of a Da-rling. I started calling him 'Da'.

Initially, I felt a lot of guilt. I hated myself for thinking about him in this way, but I had no control over what my mind made me think and dream. I kept thinking of him, I dreamt of being with him. I was bound to him in my mind. I could not find any escape from this entrapment except suicide. Twice I tried to kill myself. But I was not brave enough to go all the way. I stopped one step short and saved myself each time.

I felt like my mind had been bifurcated into two: sane and insane. But these sane and insane parts were not as social norms would maintain. They were antithetical to the social yardstick. What was sane to me was insanity to the world outside my mind, and what was insane to me was their sanity. My insane mind wanted me to be free of my desire. But my sane mind was another world. It knew no restrictions. It kept me tied to what I had seen. It motivated me to live and attain my heart's desire. Had I listened to my insane mind I would have died a long time ago. My sanity, their madness, kept me alive. However, the contradictions were too many to be solved. I thought it would be better to clean the slate once and for all. That day I locked myself into my own self, my closeted world.

For the world outside, a closet is a place to hide, to conceal one's shame, one's guilt, to live two lives, but for me it was not just a refuge but a permanent abode. It created within itself an entire universe—thousands of realities, one beyond the other, just like the infinite number of reflections in two parallel mirrors. There was so much to choose from.

Day after day I immersed myself more and more in this vast space. Sometimes it was a green pasture in spring, a million buds blossoming simultaneously, perfect for the flaneur in me, ready for a roll on the green carpet. Sometimes the dark-grey Rocky Mountains challenged me to climb up and touch the stars or climb down and drink from the molten silver elixir that passed by in the valley. At other times clouds would spread across the dark blue sky, not letting the weak orange sun look at me lying in the golden harvest of the field. Every day there was a different place to explore within this closet. I hardly had the time to eat or engage in other chores.

I fed myself on two things: memory and imagination, on impressions already made in my mind and on the ventures my mind took beyond those impressions. I saw him once and it was imprinted on my mind forever, just like the engravings on the Harappan seals that speak even today. This one impression resulted in the inception of a greater faculty within me, my imagination. Not just perceiving and seeing through the obvious, but creating what was not obvious to the common eye. I realized how powerful my mind was; I began to acknowledge its true worth. I would talk to him endlessly, walk hand in hand with him, reciting to him the poetry I wrote with him as my muse, or just watch him unblinkingly for hours. My closet was shared by an apparition, his apparition. Only his touch could bring his self into my world. I began to wonder how I could attain Midas's touch.

10

The touch of a hand on Avik's shoulder made him shudder. He turned around to find Sonu signalling to him that it was time for him to leave. Neither Ananki nor Avik had noticed the passage of time. The cold food on the plate kept just beside the bars indicated that Sonu had come down with a tray of food for Ananki, but both of them had been oblivious to his presence. However, it was time for Avik to leave Ananki and her story.

As Avik turned to follow the attendant, Ananki stood up and looked him in the eye.

'Will you come again?' she asked.

'I will,' he replied.

As he walked towards the stairs, he wondered if he would really come back to listen to a girl who had not just crossed every limit but had also labelled her transgression as love.

Parents' love for their child is one of the purest forms of affection. There is nothing more sanctified than a parent-

child bond. The selfless love of parents for their offspring is often quoted as an example of how love should be; such is the nature of this bond. And there stood this girl, who calls herself a daughter, but thinks about her own father in such an unethical way, Avik ruminated as he began climbing up the stairs. Suddenly, something struck him and he rushed back to her.

Panting for breath he blurted out, 'Did your mother find out about your feelings?'

Hearing this Ananki retreated towards the dark wall, picked up her piece of charcoal and started writing on it, leaving him standing there with no answer.

It is not easy to solve the maze of her self.

Not only would he would have to sink into her depths but his descent would have to be bit by bit, like the slow-moving sun sinking into the sea, colouring the blue with its red gloss. But then some colours are immune to others, black, for instance. No matter how hard one tries, one cannot change black into another colour completely, and only a hue can be attained after much effort.

I want to see that hue within her. Until then I will have to deal with the colour of the charcoal with which she fills up these walls, Avik contemplated, staring at her agile body.

He ran up the stairs and rushed through the corridor towards the exit. All he wanted to do was climb into his bed and bury his head in his pillow.

Her story had disturbed him deeply. Never in his life had he felt so giddy. Driving back home was not easy. His head was heavy, his vision blurred, his body drenched in sweat. He wanted to go to his mother's place and rest, but decided it would be best not to trouble her.

As soon as he entered his apartment, he rushed straight to the bathroom, puking thrice in ten minutes. It was as if his body was rejecting what his mind had received. Avik could not accept what he had heard from Ananki. But neither could he ignore her. His mind felt as if it had been stretched taut between two extremes, sanity and madness, so as to tear apart its very essence.

He lay down on his bed and stared at the ceiling, feeling numb. It seemed as if every feeling had been vomited out of him. A strange sense of being in a void overtook him.

Ananki's love shakes the very foundations of the love on which the world thrives. Her love is blasphemy to the world outside her closet. Is she suffering because of it? Is her madness a form of excruciation or does it give carte blanche, a cover underneath which she can act according to her own discretion, begetting her own set of rules that govern her existence in her closeted world?

He struggled not to think about her.

He was tired of her. She had invaded his consciousness for such a long time. He wanted to break free of her, of the black curls that seem to constantly coil around his neck. He wanted to rip them apart and save himself.

Without thinking, he started stuffing his belongings into his suitcase. He wanted to leave the entire mess behind him and go back to Mumbai, to the place that had given him refuge in the bleakest of times.

I feel as if nothing of my own is left within me. No matter how hard I try to get rid of thoughts of her, I cannot. She has penetrated deep within my self. I can feel her right beneath my skin, within this blue-black vein that carries the dark, impure blood; she flows within this network without knowing any barriers. I wish I could rip my veins open and set her free.

In desperation, he lay on the carpet and howled in torment. He was thirsting for someone whom he could talk to about the conflict within him. He wanted to connect with someone who could understand his state and at the same time help him come to terms with what he now knew.

He got up and went out onto the balcony in the hope of connecting with someone, something. The crowd in the street was oblivious to him. There was no sight of the moon; the stars seem to throw spears to complete his annihilation. He ran back inside and fell on the floor, as if all of his vital juices had been sucked out. He closed his eyes. Everything went silent as if the entire cosmos had died.

He woke up to find that the sun had risen twice in his absence. He could barely get up to fetch the jug of water lying on the bedside table. His head was heavy, his body pale and weak. He emptied the contents of the jug to replenish the fluids he had lost the other night. Ananki's story still revolved in his mind. He realized that he had made a great mistake by not telling Dr Neerja about what he had learnt. He decided to call her as soon as he stepped out to get something to eat.

Meanwhile, he pondered if it was really possible for a daughter to develop such feelings for her own father. He had heard stories of incest, of molestation by relatives, of the most gruesome crimes committed in a family, but this was completely new to him. He wondered if the entire story was the product of a mad mind's imagination. After all, by her own admission, her family and Radha had heard her talking to herself. Was she suffering from schizophrenia or were her feelings real? What if they were real, as real as his own existence? The thought was scary.

She loved her father, her own father. To love one's father, not as children love their parents, but as a partner, as an emotional and sexual companion, was something beyond the realm of love.

There is no doubt that she is suffering from a severe psychological problem, some sort of madness. She is mad and she is where she is because of her madness. He tried to calm his mind by labelling her as a madwoman whose mind could not recognize the essence of parenthood, who mistook a father's care and affection as something else and harboured desire for him.

Only some months ago Sahay had published a story about a father molesting his own daughter. The story was read by a wide audience who reacted to it strongly.

Strange things happen and it's important for journalists to probe into the strangeness of life without passing their own judgment. A journalist's eye should view the picture in its entirety and not just from a single dimension.

After getting back home, he decided to do some research into how common cases like Ananki's were. He found many cases where the father had either sexually abused his daughter or was sexually attracted to her. But it was rare that a daughter felt for her biological father as a sexual companion, and it was rarer that she dared to express such a desire in public.

However, he did find something of interest. An anonymous girl had posted about her feelings for her father on a help forum, asking for ways to deal with her growing sexual attraction for her father. She was in love with her own father but did not have the courage to tell anyone, except by sharing it anonymously on an Internet forum.

She had given a detailed account of her dreams and fantasies of him as her sexual partner. She would often masturbate while fantasizing about him. She felt so strongly for him that she had decided never to get married to any other man. In the world outside, he held a position of reverence, while within the space of her room he was her lover, a companion for life. In the comments section, some people had labelled her a 'whore' while others called her 'mad'.

Avik wondered how much of herself a woman hid, out of fear of societal norms that did not allow her to be what she was and share what she felt inside. He was reminded of his mother's words, 'When the maker of this infinite universe, Lord Brahma Himself, could not understand the workings of a woman's heart, how can we expect lesser men to understand them?' Perhaps she was right, he thought. The true story of a woman's mind goes with her to her grave. He was after one such story, and perhaps that story too was after him.

Avik knew he needed Khyati. Without her help, he could not move further into the labyrinth of Ananki's self.

He knew she would be upset with him for not calling her back after the kiss, but he also knew that it would not be too difficult for him to pacify her. He had always taken her for granted, and she had always granted him a part of her self after every reconciliation, only he was oblivious to it. Khyati had always been his backup plan, just like this time.

He immediately picked up his phone to call her and as always he got a prompt answer from the other side.

'Hey, I know I have been really busy but then you know that when it comes to being with someone, it's only you I can think of. Where are you right now?' Avik tried to sound as cheerful as possible.

'At home.'

He could detect the shrill note in her otherwise soft voice. He knew she was pretending to be fine when she was not.

If she is upset with me, why doesn't she just tell it to me straight?

'I am going to pick you up in half an hour. Be ready,' he told her, waiting anxiously for her response.

She could not say anything except, 'Okay.'

At least she did not decline, he sighed in relief.

Khyati's infatuation had crossed the realm of attraction and entered that of love, which was why she could not say no to him. It was the hope of a future with Avik that made this otherwise self-respecting girl bear numerous rejections from him.

Love can make us act strangely at times. The more out of reach a person is, the more we desire them. She had soothed her bleeding heart when she had found out that Avik was dating Trisha, but ever since he had returned to Delhi and had told her that there was no one special in his life, the desire to be with him had once again found wings.

She wore her heart on her sleeve, even though she knew Avik did not feel the same way about her, that he called her only when he needed her help for his case, that there was no other interest in his life right now other than a madwoman in a cell.

As always, she did her best to look good. He was right on time. The three started to map the roads of Delhi: Avik, Khyati and the silence between them.

'You want to go for a beer or just food?' he asked, breaking the silence. 'We can go to our old spot if you like.'

'No. Just food,' she replied, looking out of the window at the road that was speeding by.

The sadness in her heart made her careful, which came across as the indifference that Avik had sensed as soon as she sat in the car. It made him uneasy. He felt repentant. He stopped the car and reached for her hand, startling her. She did not want to break down in front of him. He looked at her with the sorry face that had always made her heart melt.

'What is it, Khyati?' Avik asked.

'What? It's nothing. I'm fine. Really,' she replied coldly, still not looking at him.

'I don't think you are fine. Something is bothering you. Please tell me what it is. I beg of you.' Avik held her chin and tried to turn her face towards him.

Khyati remained silent.

'I am sorry, Khyati. I should not have done it,' he blurted, half confused himself as to what he was referring to, the kiss or his indifferent behaviour.

'Done what, Avik? What did you do that you are so sorry for now?' she replied sarcastically.

'I should not have kissed you. I am sorry for it,' he said.

There it was, the truth that hit her even harder than the silence between them. She pressed her lips together in desperation.

'It's okay, Avik. You don't need to be sorry for that. It's another thing if you are sorry for treating me like your personal assistant for this stupid case, in spite of the fact that I have gone out of my way to help you, more than a friend would.'

There, she had said it; he was more than a friend for her.

'Khyati, please forgive me for being the jerk that I am. I know that I have hurt you many times in the past few days, but it was not my intention,' Avik pleaded, still trying to make her look at him.

His seeking forgiveness again and again made her angrier. She did not want his apology but his love.

'Avik.' She finally turned towards him. 'The problem is, you are so focused on your goal that you forget everything else and trample over the people who are actually trying to help you.'

A sense of guilt overcame him as he wondered if what she had said was true.

Did I really hurt her that much?

'Khyati, you are my friend and will always remain so. But at this point in my life I am not ready for another relationship. Although I recently sensed your feelings for me, I cannot reciprocate them, not because you are not worth it, but because I am not ready.'

Khyati listened to him without a word but with eyes full and cheeks wet. She had known how he felt about her all this while, but hearing it from him was more hurtful than she had thought it would be.

Avik did not know what to do except give her a hug to console her. He hoped she was strong enough to accept that he did not feel anything for her beyond friendship. He decided that this would be the last time he met her. Only distance could heal the wounds of a heart that faces rejection. But was this a platitude to ease the guilt of breaking her heart or did such healing really happen? He was not sure. Perhaps he had never loved at all. Perhaps the one great love of his life had not yet arrived, despite the fact that he had been in three relationships over a span of ten years. Perhaps he was not born to love but to dream, and his dream was the sole love of his life.

As the thought of love crossed his mind, he was reminded of Ananki. It made him shiver. He remained silent as he drove Khyati to the metro station as she had requested. After dropping her off, Avik decided to go for a walk rather than return to the apartment.

With every step he took he reminded himself that his dream to become a famous journalist was the only love in his life.

It is the only thing that will give meaning to this otherwise meaningless existence. I cannot afford love. Love has never given me anything. I have nothing more of myself to offer for love's sake.

In spite of working for ten years, he had not been able to achieve his dream, for he had never really given his all to the job, distracted as he had been by his relationships. It was time he moved away from love and towards his dream. Rejecting Khyati had been the first step towards giving priority to his dream.

Had I been the same old Avik, I would have accepted her love, even if I didn't love her. I would have given her love a chance to kindle the same emotion in my heart, just as it happened before with Trisha. I fell in love with her over time. But this Avik is a changed individual, having seen life with the magnifying glass of failure. Mediocrity is not his way of existence now and it is time to say goodbye to everything that pulls him down to the level of commoners, Avik contemplated as he walked.

Engrossed in his thoughts, Avik did not see the brick lying in front of him on the footpath and just as he stumbled upon it, he heard a shot. It came from a car that passed him on the road. As he looked at it, trying to read the number plate, the person inside aimed at him and shot once more. This time the bullet grazed his arm.

Avik ran and hid behind a nearby tree.

Had he not stumbled, he would have been dead already. The thought made him numb.

The car vanished. Passersby gathered around him as he moaned helplessly, trying to stop the blood flowing from his arm. Two young men stopped an autorickshaw and took him to the nearby hospital, calling the police control room on the way.

11

A police car was waiting at the main entrance of the hospital. It was a clear case of attempt to murder. Naaz Mehmood, the inspector in charge of the area, looked at the amount of blood flowing from Avik's wound and told him to get it treated first. Avik was taken to the emergency room, accompanied by the two young men and Inspector Naaz, who quickly took care of the formalities associated with such a case so that Avik could be attended to. He was given twelve stitches in his forearm and was admitted for the night for observation.

Meanwhile inspector Naaz asked the two young men for their testimonies as witnesses to the shooting. After the young men left, Naaz feared Avik might be attacked again, so he instructed a constable to stand guard at the door of Avik's room.

It was almost afternoon when Avik woke up to find Naaz waiting to record his statement for the First Information

Report. Avik had never been in such a situation before. With the effect of the painkillers diminishing, he felt a pulsating pain in his arm. He asked the inspector to call the nurse.

'How long will it take for my arm to heal?' Avik asked the nurse who entered with a box full of medicines.

'It might take ten to fifteen days for the wound to heal completely, provided you do not strain it too much,' the nurse replied as she changed his dressing and handed him his medication. She helped Avik sit up in bed.

'When will I be discharged?' Avik asked, labouring to sit up even with the nurse's support.

'After the doctor visits in the evening,' she replied as she made him sit and then left.

Inspector Naaz took the chair beside Avik's bed and sat down, crossing his legs.

'Were you able to see the face of the attacker?' he asked.

'No, the window was only slightly open and there was black film on the glass, despite the rule,' Avik replied.

'What make was the car? Were you able to note its number?' Inspector Naaz asked.

'It was a black Scorpio. I was too panicked to note the number', Avik said, placing his right hand over the bandage, trying to feel the extent of the wound.

'Who do you think was behind this?' Naaz inquired, noting down the details of the car.

The question initiated a circle of arguments in Avik's confused mind.

It has been only a month since I returned to Delhi after a long absence and I've already made enemies here who are after my life. Who could have done it? One thing is for sure – the person who attacked me or the one who hired an assassin is someone related to Ananki. Perhaps someone close to her, one of her family members. There is only one person in her family who could arrange such a thing. Her father. He would not want me to publish her story and dishonour the family name. I am sure Mr Rajput is the one behind this attack. Should I tell the inspector about my suspicions? If I tell him, he will question Mr Rajput about this and Ananki's case will be closed forever. What should I do? I am not even sure if Mr Rajput is behind it. Taking his name would mean the end of it all, the end of the hope of solving the mystery of Kalki's death, the end of my dream. To say or not to say? It is better not to say when I cannot back it up with proof, for the stakes are high.

'I do not know who attacked me.' Avik kept his answer short.

'Any other details you want to share?' the inspector probed for information.

'I don't think I have anything else to say. I am still in a state of shock and I am struggling to arrange the pieces of this puzzle. Give me some time, Inspector Naaz, I will come to you when my mind is clearer,' Avik replied, feeling tired. He wanted to lie down again.

'Okay. I have your address from your licence. I will send a copy of the FIR there,' Inspector Naaz said as he stood up to leave.

'The address you have is for my mother's house, inspector. I don't stay there. I am currently based in Mumbai and am staying in an apartment arranged for me by my company, as

I came to Delhi for a short assignment. Please don't let my mother know about this attack, as she will be very worried. I will come to the police station to collect my copy of the FIR. You can take down the address of my apartment and my friend Khyati's phone number; you can call her to confirm the information I have given you,' Avik looked tense as he replied.

'All right. And if you feel threatened, you can always ask for protection,' Inspector Naaz told him before leaving.

It was 4.30 in the afternoon. Avik was thirsty and hungry. He called the nurse who gave him water and ordered a meal for him from the hospital kitchen.

After eating, Avik lay down and tried to recreate the entire incident in his mind, not knowing when he fell asleep.

The sound of a man's voice woke him up. It was the doctor. He reviewed Avik's file and checked his wound. He showed him certain exercises that would ease the stiffness in his arm. He finally signed Avik's discharge papers.

After the doctor left, the nurse told Avik that someone had been waiting to take him home. She called the person into the room.

It was Khyati. She took Avik's file from the nurse, placed it along with her bag on the table, and stood in front of Avik who was still sitting on the bed. He lifted his hand, beckoning her to come near. All he needed was a hug to console him and make him feel that everything would be fine. Khyati held him in her warm embrace where he felt safe, safe from the world that had turned hostile towards him all of a sudden.

'How did you find out about what happened to me?' was all he could ask.

'Mine was the last number you had dialled. The nurse called me and told me you were injured and had been admitted here. She said that no one had come to get you discharged. So I came,' she said, handing him a packet.

'Did you tell Ma?' Avik asked as he placed the packet on his lap, trying to open it with one hand.

'No, I did not, but you should. She should know what is happening in your life. She has the right to know that you were shot. Someone bloody tried to kill you, and for what? A madwoman's story? If you have any sense left in you, pack your bags right away and leave for Mumbai. Your life is above all this mess,' Khyati said, helping him open the packet.

'My dream is above my life,' Avik said, looking at Khyati.

'Your dream can be pursued through other channels provided you have a life, provided you can walk on your two legs, provided you are able to use your hands, provided your heart and mind are functioning and not opened up by a bloody bullet,' Khyati replied, taking a shirt out of the packet and handing it to him.

'Khyati, I am not going back to Mumbai right now. Not until I have the story. And I am not going to die before that. Not until I make a name in the journalism industry, not until I make a worthy amount of money, not until people look up to me and say, that's who I want to be, that's the life I want to live.'

Khyati knew he was stubborn, she knew he would not listen to her, but as a friend – as he thought her to be – it was her duty to try to make him understand the value of his life, for himself, for his mother for whom he was the only source of hope and happiness, for her, who had fallen in love with him despite knowing that he might never develop any feelings for her.

She helped him get up from the bed and took him to the attached bathroom so he could change his clothes. She took the hospital shirt off carefully, taking care not to hurt his injured arm, and made him wear the new one she had got for him.

'How did you know I would need this?' Avik asked, surprised.

'Pretend it's your birthday gift in advance,' she smiled and left him to change into his trousers.

When he was ready, Khyati completed the discharge formalities and called a taxi. She had thought of every little thing that Avik would need and he noticed it too. He felt lucky to have a friend like her. However, he worried that she might be doing all this in the hope that her actions would kindle stronger feelings for her in him.

But his notions about love were clearer than before. Three failed relationships had made him realize that love could not be earned. It just happens, like a flash of lightning striking a tree and burning it to ashes within seconds. Such is the nature of love. It changes the entire being of the person who is struck with its arrow. It is like an illness that possesses the body and mind alike, rendering the person vulnerable. It is like a temporary madness that makes one turn a blind eye to reason and logic.

Avik cared for Khyati, he knew he would do everything he could to make sure she was safe and happy, but he could never love her.

Khyati caught Avik staring at her and asked him what he was thinking about, to which he smiled and replied, 'Thank you.'

She forced a smile in return, realizing that the verbal gesture was perhaps the only way in which he could thank her.

The taxi had arrived. She helped him get into it and, deciding it was best not to go with him as she had originally planned, closed the door gently after him.

'I would advise you to go home to Ma,' she said, almost begging him.

'You know I cannot, and promise me you will not call Ma and tell her about this.'

'I won't. But you should. She has the right to know. Take care and give me a call if you need me,' Khyati replied, standing back as the taxi pulled away.

On the entire way back to the apartment Avik kept thinking about the attack that could have taken his life. One thing he was sure of was that someone related to Ananki, someone close to her, someone who did not want him to meet her and learn her version of Kalki's death, was behind it. Once again, he could think of only one person: Mr Rajput.

No one else would have a problem with my meeting Ananki to learn the truth in order to publish her story. I am sure it's him. What concerns me is why he doesn't want Ananki's version to be published. Is it just because of the family's honour or is there some other reason? Does Ananki know something about her mother's death that she should not? Was Mr Rajput responsible for his wife's demise? Did he get involved with his daughter? Did he kill his wife because she found out about it and is he now after my life for trying to unravel the mystery behind Kalki's death? Whatever his reason is, it was him, Avik concluded as he entered the apartment.

Tired, he took his medication and went to bed. He soon fell asleep.

12

In Ananki's cell, her lean hands turned black from wiping the charcoal off the walls. It was a ritual practice that completed her day and welcomed the arrival of dusk. In contrast to Avik's response to their meeting, Ananki appeared quite composed. Her breath was gentle, her posture was relaxed and there were hardly any frown lines on her face.

Avik's question – did her mother find out about her feelings for her father – should have disturbed her as much as her story had disturbed him. But she had grown accustomed to accusations of every kind that had come her way ever since her mother had died. Nothing bothered her now. Nothing could break through her shield of non-responsiveness, not even him.

She wanted to meet Avik again, not to speak to him but to hear from him about the world outside, the world where Da lived. She wanted to feel the air Da breathed, fill her nostrils with his scent once more. She wanted once again to see the land where he walked tall and gracefully. It had been a long time since she had last seen or heard from him.

All this while he had existed either as an apparition of her memory or as a figment of her imagination. She had missed seeing the real him, 'the handsome man who could give an inferiority complex even to the gods, such was his stature and grandeur', according to her.

The last time she had seen him was when he had brought her to Dr Neerja's NGO, to get rid of her. A pearl of sweat seated at his temple – although it was mid-January and the Delhi winters were at their peak – proved the amount of passion he had within him, if only he could share it with a woman other than his wife. His deep dark-brown eyes had watched Dr Neerja intently as she spoke to him, as he nodded in consent to whatever she told him. His lips seldom moved except twice during the entire conversation, in the beginning to greet the doctor and at the end to say goodbye to her.

He did not say goodbye to me, nor did he look at me one last time. I was shattered seeing him leave me in this terrible world all by myself, she remembered.

Avik did have some effect on her. How and to what extent, she could not fully understand. He was the second man who had shown kindness to her, despite knowing who she was. Although she had nothing more to say to him, she wanted to see him again. Telling him anything else would mean allowing him entry into her dark world; she preferred him just outside it, neither too near, nor too far away, in a space that belonged neither to her nor to him. In that space she wanted to meet him. Ananki closed her eyes to allow utopian dreams to float through her mind.

There is nothing more calming than walking barefoot on the wet green of a vast pasture. I have never felt at such ease before in my life. I have been walking here for a long time, yet I do not feel even the slightest fatigue. The sight of golden-bearded barley in the faraway corner of this flat earth makes me walk at a fast pace.

I am almost running now, but the barley field seems to be at the same distance as it was when I started. I look at my long, lean legs with a sense of wonder, thinking what might be the secret behind their endurance. All I know is that they take me somewhere I should be, to a place where I should have been long ago.

My body does not feel any pain, but I am feeling very thirsty. I move where my intuition leads me, walking about seven kilometres across the green pasture towards the bearded barley. My dried nostrils can smell water somewhere, not too far from where I am. I inhale deeply and then move towards the right.

A great orange ball is right in front of me now, turning to a deep red with time. The entire canvas is now covered in a bright orange hue. I have reached the corner of the earth where it meets the orange. I move into it, flip and reach the other side. There is no green or gold here, only orange. Orange grass, orange trees, orange flora and fauna and amidst them an orange lake. I run towards the lake, wanting to drink its sweet orange nectar. Drawing close, I see a huge orange scallop in the middle of the lake. For the moment I ignore it and gulp down the nectar, drinking as if my thirst is as old as the blazing ball itself, as if I will never get to drink anything ever again in my life. My being is bathed in orange. The more I drink, the more tired I feel, making me confused. The nectar should energize me. On the contrary, it is sucking out the energy that I have. All I want to do now is lie beside the lake and rest, rest timelessly underneath the great orange tree on its banks. My eyes drift shut, but I can still see that scallop in front of me, floating over the orange lake.

Suddenly the scallop begins to open, emitting deep purple rays that reach the horizon. The purple is filling me with my life source. I get up and move towards the source. I stay on the shore, for I can't swim. I sit there waiting for the scallop to open completely, expecting a pearl to be born from within it. I feel like my spirit has been waiting for this pearl for centuries. Just like a phoenix that rises from its own ashes, it has been sitting here since my childhood to my death, coming back again and again to complete the wait. I do not remember how many cycles have passed, but something within me tells me that this might be the last cycle, that the wait might be over, that I might have been heard this time.

The scallop opens, throwing out a spectrum of light that makes the surroundings glow with the seven most beautiful pastel shades I have ever seen. Something emerges from the scallop. A female figure hovers over it. I cannot see her face, but I feel she is familiar. She looks like a newborn babe, born fully grown though, each and every curve of her body showing forth its new-found splendour. I can see her stretching her arms upwards as if awakening from a long sleep.

A thousand purple butterflies leave her tresses to find a different abode, oblivious of the fact that they won't be able to *find a better haven than this fragrant harbour. As she lifts one of her feet to step out of the scallop, her tresses coil around her nether parts to save her from any shame. Her countenance, though, is free from any shame or guilt.*

Perhaps it is I who feel shame watching her secretly like this. She tiptoes over the lake, stepping carefully so as not to disturb the placid water, and moves towards the shore. It is better that I hide myself behind a bush. I do not want to confront such a sublime beauty; I feel like a naught in front of her.

She seems to be looking for someone. Her eyes measure the vast orange canvas in search of something.

My heart is beating really fast now because of the fear of being found out. I press my hands hard against my mouth and nose in order to stifle the sound of my breathing. She walks past me without noticing me. I sigh in relief. I am tempted to follow her, but what if she sees me? I would die of embarrassment.

She plucks the brightest fruit from the tree and gorges on it. While she satiates her hunger, I watch her eat with hungry eyes. She whispers something in the ear of the huge orange-coloured tree, smiles and closes her eyes. I have never been so curious in my life.

From the trunk of the orange tree, a young boy appears in front of her. He seems to be her long-lost counterpart, covered only in what nature has given him, a thick pelt of hair across his chest and pelvis. I move a little closer to get a better look at his face, but I cannot see it. She is obstructing my view. She looks at him. Their eyes meet and hearts conjoin as if a heavenly union is about to take place. I have seen both of them somewhere, although I cannot remember where. I feel I know them. I feel I have known them for a very long time.

He holds her by her waist and pulls her close to him. Her tresses coil around him in order to fuse him with her, into her. I turn my back to avoid being a voyeur but cannot help myself on hearing the sound of dried leaves rustling beneath their bodies. She lies under him, brimming with the joy of his presence. A million petals fall over them, spreading the most enticing fragrance around them. But more distinct is the smell of their spirits that flow from one into the other through the first kiss. It is an eternal smell that belongs only to them, their union. The smell is intoxicating. It has a deep, wet effect on me. I try hard to ignore the overbearing feeling and concentrate on what my eyes see. I am waiting for the kiss to end, but it does not. The more I hope it ends, the more passionately they conjoin.

Their bodies gleam with the unity of their spirits. They emit a lot of heat, as if they have produced their own sun, melting everything around them. Purple fluid spreads underneath them. It binds not only with the two spirits but also with the spirit of nature, leaving a mark of their form on this infinite formless universe. They are melting into each other. Within seconds their bodies vanish and only the life source is left, ready for a sacred amalgamation with nature. The purple mixes into the orange, forming a pur-ange colour. Now their essence is eternal.

Out of their molten selves emerges a purange-coloured body, half-male and half-female, the masculine and the feminine energies of the universe in an inseparable form. For a few seconds, nature seems to glow with the aura of this magnificent figure. It moves towards the orange lake and vanishes into its depths. I run towards the lake, but it is too late to catch a final glimpse of the glory. I look into the lake and find that the water goddess was no other than my spirit.

I run towards the tree that just witnessed a wonder. The flowers, the fragrance, the glow, everything has dissolved along with the figure. I call out to my soulmate, the one who unified with me moments ago, but I do not get an answer this time. Disappointed, I sit alone under the huge tree and close my eyes. I can see him, the man who mated with the water goddess. I recognize him. He is Avik.

13

In his room, Avik woke up with a sense of utmost fulfilment. He felt as if his spirit had left his body to drink from the eternal vial of life, as if the source of his existence had pulled him for a cosmic union with its soulmate, something he had never experienced before. It was as if he had woken up from darkness to a moment of unfading luminescence.

He went out onto the balcony and sat there, straining to recollect the details of what he had just experienced. Was it a dream or an astral projection? He felt one with a celestial being, merged with her essence in a timeless cosmic unity.

Perhaps it was just a weird dream, Avik thought as he scratched his head in bewilderment, trying to collect and fuse together the broken pieces of the dream and make sense out of it.

I certainly saw my spirit uniting with a female spirit, like two lost parts of a whole coming together after a separation of a million light years. It gave me a sense of completeness I have never experienced before. Not with any of the women I have been with. But who was the female spirit in my dream? Was it Khyati? Is my mind trying to tell me that she is the one I should be with for all the love she can give me? But it couldn't have been Khyati. I do not feel it was Khyati. Avik closed his eyes as he tried to remember his other half from his dream.

No, it was definitely not Khyati. She does not evoke the same response as I now think about her. Had it been her, I should have felt the same completeness I felt when I woke up. Was it Trisha? I certainly do miss her at times, but it was not Trisha either.

Avik closed his eyes once more to probe his mind and saw the spirit in front of him, her back to him. *Yes, there she is.* He asked her to turn around to face him, filled with a strange fear, as if his intuition had already told him who she was. His fear came true.

Ananki? No! It can't be. How can someone feel such completeness because of someone who is so incomplete as far as being human is concerned? This is a trick that my mind is playing on me. It must be a sign, a warning to guard myself against her insane self, which can drive me into it and make me as insane, locking me within her closet for the rest of my life. I should be more careful in her presence.

Avik felt exhausted by his search for the identity of the female spirit; he went back inside and lay down on his bed, soon falling asleep.

When he woke up he did not remember anything, not even his own words of caution. The diminishing effect of the medicines had brought back his rational consciousness but along with it a lot of pain. The doctor had advised him to rest for at least a fortnight, but he could not waste that much time doing nothing about the case. At the same time, his injury made it difficult for him to move about. He decided to call Sahay.

Mornings had always been the best time to talk to him, before his good mood – the result of a night of great sex, most likely – was washed away by the happenings related to a hundred deadlines at the office.

'Good morning, Avik. How have you been? So what is the secret behind Kalki's death? I am sure you must have pulled it out of that tigress's mouth by now. I can't wait to be the second one to know the details and make them known to the world. And trust me, the story will be huge,' Sahay bombarded him even before Avik could say hello.

This was what Avik hated the most about Sahay. He did not care to listen to others.

'I am still working on it,' Avik interrupted.

'What? Why is it taking so long?' Sahay asked.

Avik noticed the sudden change in Sahay's tone. He didn't like it, but it was important for him to burst his euphoria and show him the real picture of this seemingly simple case.

'I was shot day before yesterday,' Avik told him.

There was silence at the other end.

'Are you there?' Avik asked.

'Yes,' Sahay replied after a pause, then continued, 'How did this happen? Are you all right? Who do you think might have done it?'

'I was lucky. I stumbled just as the person shot at me and the bullet only grazed my arm. Else it might have gone right through my heart. I am not sure who did it, but I will find out. I have filed an FIR,' Avik replied.

'Come back if you want to. There are several other stories you can work on. I don't want to put your life at risk just for a story.' Sahay sounded worried.

For the first time in all the years that Avik had been working for Sahay, he sensed concern, something very unusual from a man like him.

Avik was adamant on remaining in Delhi, but he asked to be moved to an accomodation near Dr Neerja's NGO, so that he did not have to spend the majority of his time and energy commuting. Sahay, unlike the previous time, agreed at once and asked Avik to check into a hotel of his choice. One incident had changed the way Sahay had been treating him all these years.

It took Avik a day to pack and move to the hotel he had selected. He was tired, and in a lot of pain. All he wanted was a long, dreamless sleep.

Avik felt a little better the next morning. His mind was refreshed but his body was tired, and he was still in a lot of pain. His tired body wanted him to rest for a few days, but his mind wanted to talk to Ananki. As always he listened to his mind and got out of bed.

Avik wanted to draw on some positive energy to overcome the pain and fatigue his body was feeling, so he closed his eyes and thought of his mother's chanting. It worked like meditation for him, bringing a smile to his face, calm to his body and peace to his mind.

He got ready to go out to pick up the copy of the FIR, but as soon as he took his medicines, the dizziness returned. He knew that no matter how hard he tried, his body was not ready yet. He would have to rest for at least a few days. He called Inspector Naaz to ask if the copy could be sent over to him. The inspector suggested that it was better he sent someone to collect it. There was only one person who could do that for him. He asked Khyati to collect the copy and keep it with herself till they met.

Avik knew his next visit to Ananki would be loaded with the power of nemesis, for both her and him. He would go to any extent to get her story, but it was essential that he develop a strategy in order to do that, for beneath that madwoman's mind lay a cunning contriver who could make all his efforts turn to ashes. It was best that he utilized these days of rest to formulate a plan that could help him succeed in his endeavour.

Building trust is essential to the accomplishment of my goal. What can I do to win her trust so that she confides in me the truth that lies buried in her heart? He kept pacing in his room, pondering over and juggling between the various options his mind threw at him.

What approach would work best for a girl who had gone mad for love's sake? It was love that could work. The thought had made him shudder earlier, but today was a different day altogether. Today he would look through her madness using her own tools. He was not sure if he would get through the door of her closet, but he knew he had the apparatus he needed to work with.

While working on his strategy, his mind was filled with questions, more than he could answer. Out of all them, one question kept resurfacing.

Who was the hunter and who was the hunted? Did any such binary exist between them? What if in his hunt for the story he became the hunted? What if he was stuck in this game eternally?

Am I ready to put my entire life at stake for a madwoman, a woman who loves someone else to the extent of madness? What if in this enactment of love I forget that I am actually playing a part?

His thoughts went from being confined to the question of his role to the larger question of the roles people play in society. He took out his pen, fetched a sheet of paper and began to scribble down his thoughts. The written word had always given him a much clearer perspective than the spoken word or thought.

'*Unconsciously, everyone starts believing in the great mask they wear while playing their part, forgetting their inner self, which contradicts the external one. Is anything true? Yes, the rocks, the sky, the earth, the trees, all these are true, but human beings are far behind such existence. Each one is a character eternally seeking an author that can give him or her directions to play their part well. On this stage called life, everyone sees himself or herself as a hero, inventing a role for themselves. This role gives meaning to their life, without which it is formless. But then the root of torment lies in other actors, who try to cast you as subordinates in their plays, imposing their own image upon you, however distorted and capricious it might be, fixing you in a formulated scene, forcing you to live inauthentically. The actor who is fully conscious of his or her role has indeed found their author.*

Avik had chosen his role, just like Ananki had chosen one for herself several years ago. Both were heroes in their own plays, and Avik's choice of merging their plays and bringing them onto one stage would lead to one of the two truths becoming false. Which of the roles would emerge as truth was hard to tell as of now, but Avik was sure that he was ready to take this chance.

Fifteen days of rest and planning had given Avik a better understanding of the case and brought a new confidence to his countenance and approach. It would soon be the most important day of his life.

Sonu had been looking for an opportunity for Dr Neerja to be absent from the NGO, even if it was for a few hours. He informed Avik as soon as she had to rush back home, as Dr Bhalla had complained about chest pain. It was unlikely that she would come back to the NGO.

On the way Avik's mind worked only on his modus operandi – professing one's love to a woman in an asylum can be quite unnerving. This would probably be the last time he would see her. He had to build a false world for her and it would not be easy to make her believe in the world constructed by him. It had to be perfect, not merely driven by his instincts and her response.

The stairs down to her cell appeared darker than usual, or perhaps it was just his nervousness that made them appear so. He walked down carefully, but the soft sound of his feet had already alerted the being caged inside.

She stood pressed against the bars, her nipples flattened by them. Her pubic hair was more prominent than usual under her ill-fitting gown that was pressed against her by the bars. Avik looked at her from a distance and stopped short. The force that had always pulled him back worked this time too, but today he felt it was feebler than usual.

I hope it can sustain me long enough to put together the pieces of the puzzle, he thought as he looked at her. The longer he stood, the faster the blood in his veins travelled straight to his groin. *Her raw sexuality can arouse even the most asexual man.*

He had never denied the strong physical attraction he felt for her. What he feared was her mind. But for the moment, he wanted to forget everything her mind had to offer and receive all that her body could give him.

He walked towards her and stood right in front of her, leaving just enough space for the air to pass between them. He waited for her reaction. No response. She did not move even an inch. The way she looked at him boosted his confidence; she stared straight into his eyes, her head cocked slightly to one side, her lips opened in a gentle pout, as if asking for something.

Without thinking for another second he reached through the bars to hold her face between his hands and pull it towards his, and then pressed his lips tightly against hers. At first, her willowy frame remained still, her hands hanging beside her thighs. But gradually he felt her thawing with the warmth of his tongue. She reached her arms out through the bars to hold him tightly by his waist, digging her nails into him. While he sucked on her lower lip, his hands moved quickly over her in the discovery of her body. Her thighs were lean, just as they looked beneath the gown; her hips were narrow, he could encircle her waist with his hands; the smoothness of her neck and the fire she had lighted in his spirit led his fingers to her small but firm breasts.

He kissed her and kissed her, until his trance was broken by the push she gave him, making him stumble back against the opposite wall. He stared at her from beneath his lashes; she reciprocated the fervour. Even if neither acknowledged it, there was definitely something between them. It had been there from the moment he had seen her as a silent shadow lurking behind these bars. It might not be love or even the hope of a relationship, but there was a connection, a spark that could send them up in flames.

Every union needs such an initial spark, be it physical attraction or an emotional connection or, if one is lucky, an intellectual kinship. This kiss had sealed the bond between the two. It was not either one's first, but neither would be able to erase it from their memory.

She was infuriated at herself and at him for what had happened, for the kiss immediately barred her from the sacred space of her ever-loyal self that had been bound only to 'Da' till now. So enraged was she that she was ready to rip him apart, tear his heart out and eat it raw, had the bars not protected him. She banged her fists against the bars, and then retreated towards the back wall till she bumped against it. Deeply hurt by the sense of helplessness, she cried loudly.

Each sob was like an arrow that pierced his chest, bringing out in him an immediate feeling of remorse.

At that moment, Sonu appeared with Ananki's lunch; he opened the door and placed the tray inside. Avik asked him to leave the door unlocked, although the thought scared him. Sonu left the lock and the key hanging in the latch and left.

Avik exhaled a deep breath and without procrastinating any further went inside the cell. Ananki sat with her knees drawn up against her chest and her arms wrapped around them, probably to shut him out of her world, but he had to invade it, no matter what. He sat behind her and held her tightly.

'I am sorry, Ananki. I had no right to thrust my feelings upon you.'

He paused. Would he really be able to deliver an impressive declaration de l'amour, something that would melt her heart and make her believe him, trust him and confide in him?

He had never been very vocal as far as matters of the heart were concerned. But was this really a matter of his heart or was it a device of his mind? Every binary was being dissolved as he delved deeper and deeper into the waters of Ananki's self. He felt a strange giddiness overtaking him, making him want to expel the words necessary for the bigger picture.

'Ananki, I want you to forgive me for what I just did. You don't know this, but ever since I saw you, I have felt a deep metaphysical connect. No matter how much I try to stay within the limits of my professional ethics, the vibes that emanate from you make me want to challenge every bar set between you and me. I know you don't really care about me. For you I might not even exist beyond these few hours of our meetings, but for me these moments have given birth to a craving for that self of yours that is untarnished by this physical world.'

He paused out of sheer astonishment at his own words.

Why had they never come to his aid when he had actually needed them, when he was facing failed relationships one after another? What had made him declare love in such an exquisite manner when he was actually repulsed at the thought of loving her?

He stood up immediately, ready to leave, to come back later to continue this dangerous game, but she clutched his hand and pulled him back to her. She held him tightly for a long time, or perhaps it seemed longer to Avik, who felt as if he was holding an alternative universe in his arms.

He had only hoped that he would be successful in winning her over, but that hope was now coming true. Terror struck him, numbing his mind, which at present was totally under her control. It was not his mind that made him lift his hand to her head but her mind that coerced his to stroke her hair and soothe her: the modern Odysseus under a perfect Calypso spell whose 'being' now belonged not to him but to her.

She reclined against his chest while he stroked her tresses and lifted her face to read the expression in his eyes – surrender. She widened her lips into a feeble smile and gave him a small peck on his lips, which smiled back at the gesture.

Perhaps the deed is done. Perhaps I will get what I came for after all. Perhaps she now likes me. No! She really does like me; why else would she bestow upon me a token of her affection? This is the time. Thoughts of success ran through Avik's mind.

He was sure he would get the real Kalki Rajput story from her own daughter, who now trusted him completely. He thought it would be best to take things to the next level, before she changed her mind.

'Ananki, you are the sole ruler of both my conscious and subconscious mind. No other woman has left a mark upon me as you have. But then, I feel I still do not know you. The only image I have of you is the one I have captured from behind these bars. I want you to remove them and show me your real self, which I believe is much more beautiful than anything I can imagine,' Avik said, planting a kiss on her curls that smelt like petrichor.

This time her smile could be seen from ear to ear. He wanted to know her. The question was which self she would show him.

She had to give him something. It was important that she reciprocate his 'love' by sharing a part of her self. Only a part, though. His request, however, made her chuckle.

'What is so funny?' he asked.

'Nothing. I just remembered something I wrote a long time ago,' she replied, picking up her diary.

'What is it? Can I have the honour of listening to it?'

'Here, read this,' Annaki said, finding the excerpt and handing her diary to him. 'I wrote it when Da told me that he would never be able to understand me. He was perhaps the only one who was honest enough to admit this universal failure.'

He took the diary from her and read.

I smile at people who say they know me or want to know me. To know me a little, one needs to stay attuned to my actions. To know me partially, one needs to keep in constant touch with my words. To know me fully, one needs to become unified with my ideas. But my ideas are not for the world to understand, and hence, neither is my self.

Her words triggered a series of questions in his mind.

'Does a person have only one self or is one's personality made up of a number of different selves? What do you think? Is the self a static entity or does it keep evolving through various life experiences?' he asked her as he stood up and walked towards the door.

'I would put it in a better way. Our self comprises a number of structural elements in any given moment of experience. The play of these elements forms the basis of our experience,' Ananki replied, holding the door that had been left open.

'What are these elements that comprise the self?' he probed further, looking at her, wondering if the elements that comprised her self were the same as those that comprised his self.

'The elements are thoughts, feelings, self-concept, self-sense and recognition. In any given experience, the intensity, duration and frequency of these elements define the self. You can google them for details. Try reading phenomenology,' Ananki smiled at him as she said this.

Ananki promised Avik a glimpse into her self, but asked him to come the next day. Avik requested her to tell him her complete story now itself, as he knew he might have to wait longer for Dr Neerja to be absent from the NGO. He knew this sneaking into her cell might not work for long, as someone might inform Dr Neerja and then it would be over for him. But he had no choice. He stepped out of the cell and turned towards her to bid her goodbye.

'Today we should let these newly discovered feelings settle down,' she said as she closed the door between them.

He kissed her forehead before turning to leave.

Time certainly was required. Not for matters of the heart, however, but for the machinations of the mind, to decide how much of her self should be revealed to him. Would she remain the same after she disclosed the essence that formed her being? Would her self remain the same tomorrow or would it change overnight? Every second every self changes, physiologically and psychologically. The environment changes our body, circumstances change the way we think. Man is really a relative being. What is he on his own? Nothing. It is this 'nothing' that defines him in isolation.

From the many negations that defined Ananki, she picked the most convincing one to narrate to him the following day. However, narration had its limitations – questions, for example. Questioning would mean challenging the reality she presented before him. She did not want multiple perspectives arising due to a dialogic narrative. The best would be to not allow him a different interpretation to the one she would put forth; she had the entire night, along with the sheets of paper and the pen she held in her hands after a long time.

Luckily, Dr Bhalla's ill health required Dr Neerja to stay with him at home. Avik got the chance that he needed so much. He came a bit earlier than usual. He was curious. He was going to know the unknown. As a token of thanks he brought flowers for her. She smiled, noticing the pink roses he carried, and came forward to receive them. As Avik gave her the flowers, the thought flashed through his mind that their meeting was a date of sorts, only the setting was a bit inappropriate.

'I would like to have dinner with you someday,' he whispered.

She giggled, telling him that it might be too much to ask from someone in her circumstances.

'I find the idea of going out to eat very stupid,' she told him.

'And why do you find it to be stupid?' he asked.

'I find it stupid because I have no interest in filling up my body. I want more from a person than just dinner and flowers and material gifts. I want music and poetry, or a close dance in dim light,' she replied, wrapping her arms around his neck.

'I will try and write a poem for you, if that would make you happy. But why don't you recite one of your poems to me?' Avik said, looking into her eyes. He noticed for the first time how long her eyelashes were.

'I will introduce you to the world of my poetry when the time is right, when I feel that you are ready to read and immerse yourself in it,' Ananki replied.

'Is there anything I will be able to know about you?'

'Yes, you will know the story that you came for,' she said, handing him several sheets of paper. 'Sit here with me and read this. This is all I could manage. Read it aloud, please.'

Avik took the sheets from her, sat on the floor just beneath the dim light bulb and started reading out loud.

14

The grey in his hair made him look more appealing than ever. She, on the other hand, had lost most of her charm. Her face had wrinkled, her breasts sagged. The stretch marks and flab were prominent whenever she wore a saree. But he still loved her, loved her with all her imperfections, and loved her for all her imperfections. It was something that would never change, something that tortured me every single second of my life.

At night when he closed the door of their bedroom, my mind would suffer as if it was being roasted over the eternal flames of hell. His oblivion stood as a one-way mirror between us, he never cared to see my passion for him through it, whereas I watched every single move of his. The more I saw, the more I burned myself. Someone rightly said, 'Ignorance is bliss.' Till the time I was oblivious to the complications of this triangle, my life was simple. But then simplicity was not what I chose for myself.

Dad's fiftieth birthday was approaching. He did not want a party, but a small family celebration, so despite her wishes my mother instructed the cook to prepare dinner at home. I had baked a cake for him and wanted him to cut it at midnight. It was a surprise. I had not even involved Priyanka in it. I wanted to be the sole owner of the smile it would bring to his face. As far back as I could remember, Mom had never cooked anything for him. She was not made for such chores. How little she knew him. How could she know him when I did?

I knew how much he cherished such acts of affection. But when I took my piece of affection to him, I found him showering his on his useless lovely wife, my mother. Unfortunately, I had to be a witness to their act. There he was, mounted on top of her while I stood behind the half-closed door. As I watched, I became more interested in observing her than him. He was fabulous. She, on the other hand, looked like a lump of flesh withstanding the force of her husband who, by his vigour, seemed half her age.

Initially I thought of leaving my present at the door, but then he would know that I had been there. I did not want that, at least not for the time being. I went to their door again the night after to check if it was open. Yes it was. It became regular for me to visit their room and watch them. The more I saw him, the more I wanted to be in her place. Every day my mind would think of ways in which I could take her place. The sinner in me started to hope for it to happen someday. And then my hope came true. One day I got my chance. Mom had to go away on an urgent business trip. Dad was in Paris and was returning that night after a month. She asked me to tell Dad, since his phone was not reachable. Priyanka had gone on a school trip. It was my day (night).

I wore her red nightgown. When I looked in the mirror I could not believe it was me. I was not lean like I am today. I was full-figured and looked very sexy in that nightgown, only I could not let him 'see' me in it. I was dancing with joy at the thought of what the night might bring when I heard his car. I quickly switched the lights off and slid under the blanket. I could hear his footsteps and my heart started thumping in nervousness. What if I was caught? That day I realized that sanity makes you a coward while madness gives you courage. My madness for him gave me the courage to go beyond every limit society has set for us.

The moment he entered the room I could tell from his gait that he was drunk, which made me less nervous. He fell into the bed beside me and was about to pass out when I made my move. I could not let the opportunity go to waste so I started caressing him. At first he was taken aback. I stopped to allow him to follow suit. Less was more. Had I continued, he would have known that it was not his wife beside him that night. I had charged him just enough to take me on. I had to receive all that he offered, silently, just like her. I wanted to shriek, moan like a mad bitch while he stroked me, but I did not. I kept it all inside, buried it deep within myself and left early in the morning.

I fell asleep with a great sense of accomplishment but woke up with a sense of loss. He had made love to me thinking I was her. It was important for me to let him know it was me. There was no end to my mind's wants. When I did not have him, all I wanted was to lie with him; when that happened, I could not digest the fact that he did not know it was me he had made love to. I should have been happy about it, even waited for more such opportunities, but my madness would not let me. I was adamant that he know it had been me and not his wife. I wrote it all in a letter and posted it to our address. I wanted to use last night's act as the means of their separation.

Ananki made him pause at this point, reached for her diary and took out a letter. It appeared old and crumpled. She unfolded it and read it out to him.

Da.

For eighteen years, if I have done anything apart from surviving in this closeted world of mine, it has been to love you with all my mind and spirit. Last night was very special to me. I do not regret the path I chose to reach you. As they say, all is fair in love and war. Moreover, treachery and cunning are not new to a woman's vocabulary. I am writing this letter to let you know how fascinated by you I have always been and despite your indifference towards me, I did have you last night. When you slept in my arms after consummating our holy bond, I felt I had attained everything I had ever desired. Did you mistake me for her or did you realize it was me beneath you? Well, if you don't know, it was me whom you pierced last night, not her. You can never free yourself from this act of love, caught with me in this mirrored closet, and I shall keep you locked with me inside it forever. It is an infinite universe with innumerable alternative realities for you to chose from, one behind the other. I now stand in this vast unfathomed space, touched by you, kissed by you and loved by you. You will think of me as the betrayer and I would think the same of you, but that will not change what has already happened. I know you cannot love anyone else till your beautiful old wife breathes, but the truth of last night shall prevail forever. Last night you betrayed her and yourself. All I need to know now is when you will bring her face-to-face with it. Or do you want me to do it?

Yours only
A.

Avik wanted to ask her something but she hushed him, telling him to finish reading without interruptions. He nodded and carried on.

Somehow Da had no time to read his mail in the morning before he left for his office and instead of him the letter reached the hands of my mom. She was infuriated. Luckily, I had not typed my name, just my initial and she, stupid as she is, could never imagine it was me who was behind it. She thought Da was having an extra marital affair and kept brooding over it all day, not calling him even once, so that she could confront him face-to-face and read his expressions on being caught.

As soon as he came home that evening, he was served with questions right at the door. Shouting at the top of her voice, she asked him who he was sleeping with. He told her again and again that he was not sleeping with anyone, but she would not listen to him. I had seen them fighting many times before, but this time her tone was different, very unusual. She was deeply hurt. He was no longer interested in her. Without seeking an explanation she yelled at him without pause. He was aghast at her words and had nothing more to say, for she was adamant in her disbelief. After all those years of faithful worship, he got suspicion in return. His eyes fell on the paper she had been holding all that while; he pulled it from her grasp and read it.

'Oh, so you have faith in a random letter and not in me, who has never looked upon any woman except you, who has never thought of any woman except you, who has never cared for any woman except you. All these years it is you whom I have loved, through thick and thin, and this is what I get in return? You believe this crap and not me. Fantastic! It shows how much faith you have in this marriage. If you really think it to be true, you can do whatever you want and I will accept it. I have nothing more to say.'

As he said this, tears rolled down his cheeks, making my mother's tender heart melt and she hugged him. I had failed. Not only had I failed to pull them apart, I had also brought tears to him, a greater failure than the unsuccessful separation. I could not sleep for nights after that incident. Round the clock my mind invented ways to tear their beautiful marriage apart.

I could not stand the thought of them happily cuddling in their bed every night. I was looking for the right opportunity. I thought of writing her a letter, this time signing my full name.

Mom,

I have nothing to say to you except a simple fact of my life: I love your husband. The letter you found was written by me.

Ananki Rajput'

On reading it, the first thing she did was to grab me by the throat. I smiled. What else could I do? My smile provoked her all the more. She grabbed my hair and started pulling me towards the gate of our house.

'What did you do with him, you shameless girl?' she shouted.

'Everything,' I replied as I was being dragged.

'Everything? Did you sleep with him?'

'You are old enough to understand what "everything" means. I don't have to elaborate every single detail of our lovemaking,' I said, holding my hair to ease the pain from the pulling.

She stopped and slapped me.

'When did you do it?' she howled.

'When you had gone for your business trip,' I said, looking at her.

'Did he know it was you?'

She had to ask me at least four times before I could reply.

'I don't know,' was all I could say.

She did not ask any further questions. All she wanted was to throw me out of the house. I stood there silently, smiling at her. My smile offended her. She put me in her car and drove. Drove like a madwoman. She wanted to know more about that night, my night. She insisted on every detail. I just smiled. She could not handle it. I realized that she was driving far above the speed limit. We were racing across a bridge when suddenly she turned the steering wheel to the extreme left.

She looked at me and smiled. I cannot forget the look on her face. She wanted to kill me, push me out of the moving car into the river. I thank my reflexes for making me open the door and jump out of the car as soon as I saw her swerve to the left. Her car broke through the barricades along the side and fell into the Yamuna. Failing to kill me, she had killed herself. No one ever came to know why, not even Da. You are the only one to know the truth, but I request you to let it be unknown to the rest of the world.

As he finished reading the story of Kalki's death, Avik seemed to have forgotten the questions he wanted to ask her. All he could ask was if he could keep the sheets of paper.

'You can take the story with you, but within your mind only, and you must promise me that you will keep it buried deep in your mind,' Ananki replied and tore the sheets of paper while he looked at her seriously.

'I promise,' he replied.

He felt the words came out of his mouth of their own volition, as if under her spell.

Is this the same spell that she cast over other journalists too? Did she ask them to keep her story a secret? he wondered as he stared at her, not knowing what to do.

Ananki and Avik went silent for a while. To break the awkwardness of the silence that followed the story, Avik thought of asking her if she would ever want to come out of this place. But it was Ananki who asked something first.

'Will you come back to see me?' she asked.

'If fate permits.' Avik gave her a faint smile and left.

What will I give Sahay now that I have promised her that I will not reveal her story? The question reverberated in this mind over a thousand times.

Sahay was not the kind of person who would accept nothing easily and Ananki was not the kind of woman who would let him leave the closeted space she was so obsessed with as and when it pleased him. He was trapped.

Before sleep dulled his memory, he wanted to write down every word that he remembered of the story Ananki had told him. He switched off his mobile phone to avoid being disturbed, opened a new Word document on his laptop and typed at a quick pace. The questions that had escaped his mind while he was with Ananki now came back to him. As he typed them out he realized he could not have asked them, at least not at that point of time.

Asking her how she could do what she did to her own family would have been pointless. He was sure that even if he had asked her, she would not have found the question important enough to reply to. Reason was not something she cared about, so how could he expect her to give him a reason for her actions? Madness was the only form of reason she was aware of.

'*It was indeed Ananki Rajput's madness that destroyed the Rajput family.*' Avik typed the concluding line and saved the document. He edited it twice, adding and deleting information as he found necessary. For a while, he struggled with the decision of whether or not to mail the document to Sahay. He could not bring himself to share the document, at least for the time being.

15

Avik had achieved what he wanted. He could pack his bags, catch the next flight to Mumbai and leave without anyone having the slightest inkling of his doings in the cell. Instead, he decided to go to Ananki's home to meet Mr Rajput. There were two motives behind meeting him. Firstly, Ananki's story required confirmation and only her father could give it. Secondly, Avik thought that he had procrastinated enough. He had to confront Mr Rajput about the attack.

He called Dr Neerja to request her to set up a meeting with Mr Rajput. Without her help he would not be able to even see Mr Rajput's toe, he knew.

Avik told Dr Neerja that since he could not get Ananki's story, at least she could help him get an appointment with Mr Rajput so that he would not return empty-handed. Dr Neerja seemed reluctant at first, but Avik's persistent requests made her give him her secretary's number. She told him that she would ask her secretary to fix an appointment and in case he didn't receive her call regarding the same, he could call her.

Dr Neerja's secretary called him back in the evening to confirm the meeting. Mr Rajput had agreed to it on the condition that the questions Avik asked would be related only to his wife and her death. He would not entertain any questions regarding Ananki or her illness.

'But how can I keep the conversation strictly related to Kalki?' he blurted on impulse, feeling cheated, but quickly regained his composure, knowing that he couldn't show that he already knew Ananki's story.

'Sir, you have no choice but to grab the opportunity. Do not ask him anything about Ananki,' she instructed him before hanging up.

Avik was not happy with the condition, but he was not in a position to miss the opportunity to meet Ananki's father.

When Avik arrived at the Rajput family's bungalow, he was escorted inside the house by one of the domestic staff. He entered the huge drawing room as quietly as he could. The walls were the colour of ivory and hung with numerous paintings of all sizes. *He must be a great admirer of art,* he thought as his eye fell on a huge painting on the opposite wall. It was by M.F. Husain. Till now he had only seen reproductions of the work. He wished he could touch it, feel the texture of the paint under his fingertips. His thoughts were interrupted by his escort, who announced his arrival to Mr Rajput.

Ananki's father was sitting on one of the four huge couches that formed an open cornered square at one end of the drawing room. Avik could not see his face yet, as he was sitting with his back to him. His hair was not completely grey; Avik noticed the black amidst it. It was the same colour and texture as Ananki's hair. He walked towards the couch, crossing a mahogany dining table on the right.

Avik could smell cigar smoke as he approached Mr Rajput. He came to a halt beside him and put forward his hand for a shake, but Mr Rajput asked him to be seated instead. Avik forced a smile, but Mr Rajput did not return it. He had hardly smiled since Kalki's death. Her death had changed him, causing his life to revolve in an infinite circle of emptiness, which was clearly reflected on his face.

Ananki is an exact copy of her father, Avik thought as he looked at his face with astonishment.

'How can I help you, Mr—?' Mr Rajput asked him, puffing out a large cloud of white smoke.

'I am Avik, a journalist with *The Real Times* magazine. I have been trying to learn the true version of Mrs Rajput's demise and since you were closest to her, your story matters the most.'

Avik controlled his urge to jump straight into verifying Ananki's version or asking about the attack. He wanted to build a more comfortable rapport with the man before bringing up those questions.

Mr Rajput got up from the sofa and went to stand in front of the painting by Husain. He stared at it intently for a while, puffing on his cigar.

'This was Kalki's favourite. She was a huge fan of Husain sahab. I gifted it to her on our tenth wedding anniversary. Often, when we would sit here, exactly where you are sitting right now,' he pointed to the space beside Avik and continued, 'she would explain the intricacies of this beautiful piece of work. I did not understand much, but I loved to hear her speak.'

Mr Rajput's eyes were moist, partly from the smoke and partly from the absence that troubled him night and day. He turned back towards the painting to avoid Avik's gaze.

He's a man of memories, Avik thought.

'I know it must be hard for you to cope with the loss and would like to apologize for the torment I am forced to inflict on you by asking about her death. How do you think she died?'

Mr Rajput did not turn around or answer. The only motion visible was the rising of the thick clouds of smoke from his cigar.

Avik asked another question in the hope of getting an answer from him.

'What kind of woman was Mrs Kalki?'

Mr Rajput turned around and walked back to the couch to sit opposite Avik. He loved talking about her, which was what made him entertain all the journalists who wanted to write about her.

'Kalki was a beautiful woman, both inside and out. She had a strong mind teamed with an equally strong will to achieve. There was grit in her character that was rare. She faced many ups and downs in her life and came out of every hardship a winner. As far as determination to solve life's hardest problems was concerned, few could beat her; that was what I loved about her, her never-give-up attitude.'

'But after she died, most people concluded that she had committed suicide. This seems antithetical to the kind of person she was, according to you,' Avik probed, trying to confirm Ananki's story without revealing too much of what he knew.

'I know many people believe that she committed suicide due to some family issue, but I don't believe it to be true. According to me it was an accident,' Mr Rajput said, looking at him intently.

Avik was sceptical but did not let it show on his face. Only yesterday Ananki had told him that Kalki had committed suicide, knowing she could neither live with Mr Rajput nor without him after she believed he had betrayed her. Mr Rajput's comments presented the events in a different light. He did not know whom to believe.

'Pardon me, but some people accuse you of murder, saying that you were having an extramarital affair and when your wife found out about it, you had her killed,' Avik emphasized the last few words in an attempt to hint at the attack on him as well.

Mr Rajput clenched his left fist on hearing the accusation. His eyes widened and despite the air conditioning, there were droplets of sweat shining on his forehead. For a moment it appeared to Avik that he would get up and smack him across his face. But he did not.

'I did not have an affair with anyone. I could never have killed her. I love her. I have nothing more to say,' Mr Rajput said with finality as he extinguished the cigar, his expression changing from shock at the accusation to a silent, painful acceptance of the fact that Kalki was no longer a part of his physical reality.

Avik could not tell from Mr Rajput's expression whether he was guilty of the assault or not. He decided to ask about the shooting in a more direct manner.

'Mr Rajput,' he paused to ensure that he had his full attention, 'I have been meeting your daughter Ananki in order to learn her version of Mrs Rajput's death. A fortnight ago I was shot on the road; the attack clearly proved that someone tried to have me killed. I have been thinking a lot on who stands to lose the most if I publish Ananki's story and her version of Mrs Rajput's death, and the only person who I think might be behind the attack is you. I have informed Inspector Naaz that I am visiting you today. If I don't meet him tonight and something happens to me, it will be clear to him who tried to take my life earlier and who would benefit by killing me.'

Mr Rajput was taken aback by the accusation. For a second he stared at Avik, his furrowed eyebrows, joined in the middle just like his daughters, forming a chasm across his forehead. He did not know what to say, but fearing that his silence might prove him guilty, he looked Avik straight in the eye and said, 'I am not behind it. It's up to you to believe me or not, but I have never in my life used a gun, not even for self-protection, forget about for hurting someone else.'

The little clarity Avik thought he had gained about the case now seemed to be fleeing from him.

Mr Rajput stood up to end the meeting when Avik stopped him.

'I want to tell you what Ananki told me about her mother's death. Don't you want to hear what she said?'

Mr Rajput did not reply but sat down on the couch.

'Go on,' he told Avik and closed his eyes.

Avik told him how he had been able to make Ananki speak to him about Kalki's death, how Kalki was infuriated with the letter and wanted to teach Ananki a lesson but failing to do so, took her own life. Mr Rajput gave him a patient hearing, wanting to know whatever she had told him. When Avik finished Mr Rajput got up, turned his back towards him as if to leave, but paused, looked back and said, 'I hope you don't trust everything that she said.'

Avik's heart sank. *Have all my efforts been in vain?*

Who could he trust?

'What are you trying to tell me, Mr Rajput?'

'Why would you believe what a madwoman has to say?' Mr Rajput asked him in return, lighting another cigar.

'I don't know. I have not thought about the why part much till now. But to be honest, I did not find the cell a worthy place for her. She has decided to stay in that dungeon forever just because you chose it for her. Don't you think she deserves something better than that, especially when you can easily provide it? Don't you think her story deserves to be heard?'

'That witch does not deserve anything. She does not deserve to live after what she did.'

'Sir, I know you are deeply disturbed by your wife's death. I also know how much you loved her and I am sorry for your loss. But is it fair to hold Ananki responsible for it? As you said, it was an accident. Besides, the way she is living her life now is worse than death.'

At Avik's words, Mr Rajput stood up, held him by his arm and marched him to Ananki's room. A small closeted room, just as she had described in one of their sessions.

The grey walls were covered with pictures of Mr Rajput. Avik could see that she had frozen and saved the memories that bound them together. Old toys gifted by her father were still kept safe on a wooden shelf. A collection of books by authors he admired was placed in a row on her table. A corkboard covered in small chits of paper in various colours stared at Avik as if calling him, enticing him to read the notes. The small single bed was placed alongside a huge window that made up almost an entire wall. He could see the lush garden from the window. The roof over the bed was slanted and was made of glass. *One could sleep with the stars every night here*, he thought as he noticed the blind that could be drawn to prevent sunlight from entering during the day. In a corner a small table and chair were placed. A laptop lay on the table and he could see a thin layer of dust on it.

Every little memory associated with Mr Rajput had been kept intact in this small closet of hers. He looked at all of it with wonder, thinking of how much she loved this man. *According to society, she committed a crime in loving her own father not as a daughter should but as a lover. But in her eyes, she just loved, and this room is brimming with that love.*

Mr Rajput moved towards the bed as if to sit on it, but then pulled out the chair instead. His eyes were not filled with tears but showed some inner turmoil, as if a deeply regretful memory had just flashed before his eyes. Avik knew what perturbed him. Till now he had behaved as if he knew nothing about Ananki's feelings for her father, but the sight of Mr Rajput on the verge of an emotional breakdown moved him to speak.

'I know she loves you. She told me,' he almost whispered, sitting on the bed opposite him.

Sometimes the simplest words can have a gargantuan impact. Mr Rajput froze. Then he held his face in his palms, hiding the tears that flowed freely down his cheeks.

Avik stared at the man, not knowing what to say to console him. Till now the only man he had seen crying was himself, in the looking glass. He had always been told that tears were not for a man. He could never understand why. He had always found such solace in weeping, and he was not ashamed of this fact.

He put his hand on Mr Rajput's shoulder in a gesture of sympathy. He wanted to tell him that tears were good, that it was not his fault that his daughter behaved in the way she did. But all he could say was, 'It is okay.'

'It's not okay, Avik. It's not. One act of madness destroyed my love, my entire family. And what story did she feed you? That she loves me? She does not know anything about love. All she wanted from me was sexual gratification; my own daughter. Can you believe it? Will anyone believe me? If today

I tell anyone that my daughter tried to kiss me in this very room, people will think that I was the one who pressurized her into it, that it is I who am wrong. My character will be assassinated right away.'

'True,' Avik agreed.

'You want to know how Kalki died? Ananki is the reason for her death. She wrote some stupid anonymous letter to me, asking me to tell Kalki about something that never happened. She might have fantasized about it, that I made love to her thinking it was her mother. I also found a letter she wrote to Kalki confirming that it was Ananki I had slept with. I tried to convince Kalki of my innocence, but I guess the letter had already done the damage. Kalki changed after that.'

Mr Rajput paused for a while, keeping his head amidst his palms.

"You can ask Radha, who has been looking after her since she was a little girl – Ananki's hyperactive mind makes her imagine things that do not actually happen. She cannot differentiate between what is real and what is not. That's why she had to be treated during childhood too. I asked Dr Kaul to keep her drugged, for she kept making sexual advances on me after claiming that if it could happen once then it could happen again. I could no longer be a victim of her fantasies and declarations of love. So I admitted her to Dr Neerja's NGO, thinking that it would be better if she stays away from me. I could not prove to Kalki that it never happened. My marriage was easy prey for Ananki's dangerous mind and I lost the woman I loved. No one will ever believe that she wants me and not vice versa, because the man is always the one who lusts. No one wants to know how much I loved only one woman all my life, even after her death. Even journalists like you will not entertain it. You all want a different story to fill your columns. Fidelity is not something that sells, so you don't want to hear about it. All you want to write about is who had illicit relations with whom. I have nothing to offer you. Go and print whatever Ananki told you, she is good at generating stuff for you guys.' Mr Rajput wiped his tears, trying to hide his emotional vulnerability from Avik.

Avik was silent. Only a few weeks ago his biggest concerns had been about his job and his relationship. But today those felt like nothing compared to Mr Rajput's turmoil.

Here is a man who has everything I ever wanted: status, money, power, and yet the only things that he has to console him are his tears.

Avik suddenly felt that all the material desires for which he had embarked on this journey were pointless.

How different I am from Mr Rajput. I left my relationships behind to become rich and powerful while this man's wealth and power became meaningless after the death of the one he loved. For the first time Avik felt that he had spent his adult life in the vain pursuit of the wrong goals, and that receiving and spreading love should be the only objective in life.

'Mr Rajput, I cannot empathize with you, for I cannot even imagine what you have gone through. Seeing you today, it seems to me that I had a life I could have been content with, but I wanted more. I was always searching for something that would make me happy. But actually I left behind the essence of happiness. I left behind love and relationships that could complete my world. All I want now is to go back and collect the forfeited pieces of my life and live it as a whole. Don't worry, I am not going to publish Ananki's story.'

Avik sat on the bed as he spoke, not noticing the tears that trickled down his cheeks as he lamented a lost world of happiness. Mr Rajput was moved by the kind gesture. He collected himself and put a hand on Avik's shoulder.

'If you ever need me, feel free to call me.'

'I will. Thank you.' Avik stood up and left the room.

As he walked out of the bungalow, he thought about the fact that he would have to return to Sahay empty-handed.

No story will mean no raise. What will I have? No money, no home, no love. But maybe there is something that I can do. If I am able to convince Mr Rajput that Ananki has developed feelings for me and vice versa, then I can take her out of that cell and settle down with her. Of course Mr Rajput would be happy to see Ananki with me, as it would mean the end of Ananki's obsession that his mind is overburdened with, he thought as he slowly walked towards the main gate.

Avik stopped short of the gate, deciding that it was worth trying out his plan. He returned to the bungalow to tell Mr Rajput that he had thought of a way to make Ananki fall out of love with him.

He found Mr Rajput still sitting in Ananki's room, lost in thought. Avik's return startled him, as if he had woken him up from a deep slumber.

'Mr Rajput, I have a plan that I feel it will solve your problem,' Avik exclaimed as he re-entered the room.

'How can you solve my problem, Avik?' Mr Rajput got up and walked towards him.

'Because I think I know what your problem is,' Avik replied with a faint smile.

'And I feel that you still don't know what my problem is. Go on anyway,' Mr Rajput said, leading him towards the living room.

'I have visited your daughter several times now. We have interacted a lot during our meetings. She told me about her childhood, her experiences with you, her mother and Priyanka. She also told me about how she is different from the rest of the world as far as love is concerned. But I think she behaved as she did out of a need for love. The only person who ever cared about her in her entire life was you. So she focused all her affection and love on you, her father. Now that she has been meeting and spending time with me, she has taken a liking to me. Her feelings for you are most vulnerable at this point. Maybe we can present her with something that will make her love for you fade away,' Avik said, excited.

'And what would that be?' Mr Rajput asked him, sitting on the couch.

'A letter.'

'Letter?'

'Yes, a letter, written by you, that tells her that you are not her real father, that you and your wife adopted her because you were unable to have a baby. She told me you never lie. But this time you have to,' Avik explained his plan.

'She is correct. I have never lied in my life. How can I do it now?' Mr Rajput appeared unsettled.

'Mr Rajput, one should not think of truth or lies when things of greater importance are at stake. Even the dharamraaj Yudhishthira had to speak a half-lie in order to defeat the evil Kauravas.'

'True.' Mr Rajput paused before continuing, 'Perhaps I will also tell a half-lie, though it is against my character.'

'How will it be a half-lie?' Avik was surprised.

'It is true that Ananki is my blood, but she is not Kalki's daughter. She is my daughter from my first wife, whom my parents chose for me. We were married for a year, but complications arose when she went into labour with Ananki. She did not survive the internal bleeding after her delivery. She died a few hours after Ananki was born. I was struggling to raise Ananki along with running my business when Kalki came into my life. We fell in love. She wanted to marry me, but I had one condition, that she would never tell Ananki that she was not her real mother. She promised and never told her about it, but she could never love her as a mother. So if I tell Ananki that we are not her real parents, it would be a half-lie, as Kalki is not her real mother while I am her real father,' Mr Rajput explained.

This was another revelation for Avik.

'But how can she believe me when we also had Priyanka after her?' Mr Rajput asked.

'It can happen. Many people who adopt have babies thereafter. That is not the issue. The thing is that you are the only person Ananki loves and trusts blindly. Once her trust in you is broken after knowing you kept such a big secret about her birth hidden from her all these years, her love will falter as well. It will render her vulnerable. At such a point, I will be there to console her. It might just happen that her feelings for you would even fade away.'

After much contemplation over the language and details to be provided, the two men sat down to write the letter. Avik put great thought into the phrasing of it, for this letter would decide the fate of both of them.

Mr Rajput wrote the letter by hand and put his signature at the end. Ananki knew that signature very well. After he was done, he handed it to Avik to read through one last time, to make sure there were no chinks in the armour.

Ananki,

How have you been? Priyanka and I are fine. I hope you are recovering better than expected. I had a word with Dr Neerja regarding your condition. I also had a word with your friend Avik when he came to interview me. From him I learnt what you told him about your childhood, how this strange attraction originated. After listening to all of it I have something to tell you, something that I now think I should have told you long ago. I am not your biological father. My wife and I adopted you because we could not have a child of our own. However, a few years after we adopted you, we had Priyanka. Your mother always preferred her and that was why I was extra considerate towards you, so that you did not feel rejected. You mistook my affection for something else and developed feelings that are totally unacceptable. So now it's up to you whether you want to carry forward this seemingly shocking one-sided love story about loving a man who is as old as your father, but is NOT your father, or accept the friendship and affections of a person who will make you feel complete in every way possible.

R. Rajput

Satisfied with the letter, Avik smiled confidently at Mr Rajput before leaving. He was sure that his plan would work, but he wanted someone else to reassure him.

He called Khyati and filled her in on everything that had happened since he had been shot. She wanted to see the letter immediately. He rushed to her place and found her immersed in a book. She kept the book aside, stood up and gave him a casual hug.

'You're looking much better, Avik,' she said.

'Yes, my arm has almost healed. How have you been? The doctor advised me to rest, but you could have come to meet me.'

'I am sorry, Avik. I know I should have called.'

She could not tell him again that she was tired of being his friend that she wanted more from him, something she knew he could not give her, so she had taken the mature decision not to call him. She was not one to beg for love; she would rather be by herself.

'May I see the letter?' she asked.

Khyati looked at the letter for a long time, as if she was reading it again and again. The letter meant the end of every road that led to Avik. She knew she had lost him.

'Don't call your obsession love, Avik. Do you really love Ananki?' She finally asked, placing the letter in the front pocket of his shirt.

The question gave Avik pause. He was definitely attracted to Ananki, but was it love?

I love the way she speaks, I love her long black curls, I love her big ebony and ivory eyes, I love the scent of her breath, I love the way she moves her hands while writing on the wall of her cell, I love her taste in literature, poetry in particular. But do I really love her?

'I think so,' he finally replied.

He could see the pity on Khyati's countenance. According to her, his love for Ananki meant the end of his existence for the rest of the world. She placed the already folded copy of the FIR in Avik's pocket and gave him a final hug. It was time to bid him goodbye and shut the door.

16

Losing Khyati was a big blow to Avik. He wanted someone to call his own, even if he saw her as just a friend. It seemed he had only one option.

He called Sonu to ask if he could visit Ananki. He told him it was extremely urgent. Sonu knew Dr Neerja would not come to the NGO for another two days and making Avik meet Ananki would be an easy task. But greed led him to treachery. He knew this time he could ask for whatever amount he wished. He asked Avik to pay him ten thousand rupees.

On reaching the NGO gate, Avik handed the money over to Sonu who was already waiting for him there. He didn't wait for him to escort him and went straight to Ananki. She was standing at the door, clasping the bars, her face pressed up against them, her ears straining for the sound of footsteps. Seeing that someone was still expecting him eased his mind.

'How have you been?' he asked.

'Very well, what about you?' she said, looking into his eyes, her lips curving into a big smile.

'Just as well. I was thinking about you all night,' he stroked her hair as he told her.

'Do you wish to tell me what made you think about me all night?' she asked.

The sound of footsteps on the stairs startled them both. Avik took a step back from the bars and waited for the person to come into the faint light of the bulb in the passage. It was Sonu. Avik felt relieved. Sonu opened the door of the cell.

'Be quick. My job is at stake,' he told Avik and disappeared into the dark of the stairs.

Avik went inside and stood in front of Ananki.

'My mind kept struggling with the fact that someone like you is caged in a place like this. You should not be here. You might be suffering from a condition, but it can be treated while you stay in a decent place. I kept wondering why you do not desire to be free of this dungeon,' Avik told her, holding her face between his palms.

She could sense the despondency in his tone. She wondered if he genuinely cared for her or if it was all an act, driven by some other motive.

But if it is an act, then he would have showed such concern before knowing my story. Now that he knows everything, there is no need for such pretence. Does he doubt the authenticity of the story I told him about the suicide? she wondered as she held him in her embrace.

'There are two reasons that I do not wish to break free of this existence and move out into the sane world,' she replied.

'And may I have the honour of knowing what they are?' Avik asked as he kissed her nose.

'Firstly, I cannot go against the wishes of the person who has chosen this place for me. His wish is my command. If he wants me to spend the rest of my life here, so be it.' Ananki observed him carefully as she spoke.

'And what is the second reason?' Avik asked, keeping his face impassive.

'The second reason is more of a personal choice. I find myself more restricted in the world outside than in here. All that the so-called sane people do is thrust their definition and choices of normalcy upon those who dare to think and act differently. Most of my poems are on this theme,' she told him.

'How would I know? You do not find me worthy enough of your poetry,' Avik said, lifting her chin with his finger so he could look at her face.

She raised her eyebrows, making her eyes look even bigger, freed herself from their embrace and went to pick up her diary. She searched for a page and held out the diary, showing him the poem written on the yellow page.

'No, I want you to recite it to me,' he said.

'I have recited my poems to only one man till now,' she said, holding out the diary insistently.

He took it this time. As he read the poem, he felt sorrier for her than ever. He asked her if he could keep the poem. She tore the page from her diary and gave it to him. He kept it in his pocket and then took out the letter from his other pocket.

She was happily surprised. 'Aha, you have already started the love letter game, not bad!'

'I am not its author, Ananki. Someone else has sent it for you,' Avik said, handing her the letter.

He noticed that his words had a jarring effect on her. She knew immediately who the author was. She quickly opened it and moved to the rear wall. Avik stood where he was. He wanted her to read the letter without any distraction. As he waited for her to finish reading it, he thought of what might happen.

It is either black or white for me. Today there can be no grey patches hovering in the middle. He just hoped for the plan to work as he wanted.

She cleared her throat as she walked back towards him.

'I think you know what he has written in this letter?' she asked.

'Yes, I read it on the way,' he lied.

'Do you think it is true?' she asked.

'How would I know? But it must be true if he has written it.'

Her expression did not show shock, much to Avik's dismay; he was nervous about the success of his plan.

Her skills as an actress surpassed anything he could imagine. She did not show him the turmoil that the letter had caused within her. The information had collided with the world she had built for herself. She could act composed only because there was still hope in her mind that the letter was a lie.

'Do you really love me, Avik?' she asked him, holding his face between her palms and locking her eyes with his.

'Yes, I do, and I want you out of this place. I want you to live in the world outside, if possible with me. You do not belong here. I feel we belong together,' he replied.

'I want you to talk to Dr Neerja about it then.'

'But you have always said that you do not wish to leave this place,' Avik questioned her to gauge if she was serious about getting out.

'Yes, because earlier I had no one to leave for,' she replied.

Avik nodded. 'Very well, I will speak to Dr Neerja.'

Before Avik could bid her goodbye, Sonu came running down the stairs. He informed Avik that Dr Neerja's car had arrived in the parking outside the NGO and he must either find a way to leave the premises without her noticing or devise a plan.

Avik thought that it might not be possible for him to leave the NGO without her noticing, as there was only one exit. It was better to pretend that he had come to meet her to inform her about his meeting with Mr Rajput. Before she parked the car and entered the NGO, he rushed to Dr Neerja's cabin. He sat on the chair opposite Dr Neerja's, trying to look as calm as possible.

Dr Neerja had come for an emergency situation in another ward and went straight to the patient concerned. Avik had asked Sonu not to inform her about his waiting, as he wanted to read her instantaneous reactions on being told about the meeting with Mr Rajput.

After seeing the patient for whom she had come to the NGO she went to see Ananki. To her surprise, she noticed a lot of difference in her countenance.

Before she could say anything, Ananki said to her, 'I want to go out, doctor. I want to get out of this place as soon as possible.'

Dr Neerja was stunned but clever enough not to show it. She smiled and told Ananki that she would try her best and left for her cabin.

In the cabin, Avik had waited for about an hour but Dr Neerja still hadn't arrived. He felt an urgent need to use the washroom. Avik went inside and locked the washroom door when he heard footsteps outside and then the sound of the cabin door being locked from inside. *Must be Dr Neerja*, he thought. *But why has she locked the door*?

Dr Neerja called her husband. Avik realized she was talking on the phone. He tiptoed to the washroom door to overhear what she was saying.

'Avik has always shown a great deal of interest in Ananki. What disturbs me is Ananki reciprocating the interest…

'She wants to leave the NGO. Maybe Avik is behind this change in her decision. That is why I have always kept journalists away from her, even though it made me go to the extent of keeping one on drugs and hiring a killer for another…

'…I would not have let Avik meet her, had you not asked me to because of your assistant Khyati…

'…He crossed the limit, influencing Ananki to a great extent, which is why I had to have him shot. He was jeopardizing the arrangement I had with Mr Rajput for keeping his mad daughter. But luckily for him, he survived…

'... I am telling you, Tarun, do something about him, before he takes the goose that lays the golden egg from our hands.'

Avik froze with shock. He could not move. He decided it was best to stay hidden inside the washroom till she left.

But what if Dr Neerja finds out that the washroom door is locked from the inside? he thought.

Avik immediately put his phone on silent mode and texted Sonu.

'Dr Neerja was the one who tried to kill me. I am hiding inside the washroom while she is sitting outside. Do anything to make her leave so that I can be free,' he sent him.

Sonu was standing outside the cabin itself, thinking that Avik was briefing her about the meeting as planned. On reading his message he knocked on the door with a sense of urgency. Dr Neerja got up from her chair and opened it. Sonu pretended that he was panting, as if he had rushed to inform her of something.

He told Dr Neerja that the patient she had come for was getting out of control again and she should come to see him immediately. Saying this, Sonu went out of the cabin and ran towards the stairs that went to the first floor. As expected, Dr Neerja ran after him.

Avik got out of the cabin and briskly walked towards the NGO gate. After making an exit from the main gate, he ran as fast as he could away from the NGO, stopping only when he turned onto a side street at the end of the road. He stood there, panting for breath and recalling Dr Neerja's words. Appalled, he covered his mouth with his hand, as if preventing himself from puking. It was difficult for him to believe what he had heard. Dr Neerja was the one who had tried to kill him and all the other journalists, for she did not want to lose the huge amount of money Mr Rajput was paying her.

Shaken by what he heard, Avik sat next to a roadside lemonade stall. He bought a chilled bottle of water, opened it and poured water over his head and face in order to calm down.

After a while, Avik thought it was best that he called Mr Rajput and told him about Ananki's reaction on reading the letter.

'Mr Rajput, the plan worked. Ananki wants to come home,' Avik said.

For the next few seconds there was silence at the other end.

'Mr Rajput, are you there?' Avik asked.

He could hear a sigh of relief from the other end.

'Yes. Yes, I am here. I just don't know how to react right now. All this time, I was torn apart. I could not keep Ananki with me, but being a father I did not want her to stay in that place. I want her to live a normal life away from me,' Mr Rajput replied.

'Mr Rajput, your wish might come true but just for now, do you think you can pick her up from the NGO?' Avik asked him.

'Never. How can you even think I would go there for her? I don't want her to see me and change her mind. I will send the car and the keys to my other house. Take her there. I will send Radha there to take care of her. No matter how much she insists, do not bring her here.' Mr Rajput was adamant.

'Mr Rajput, I cannot talk to Dr Neerja about releasing Ananki. You have to go to the NGO,' Avik replied.

'I will call her and tell her to send Ananki with you. She won't have any objection after she hears from me.'

'You don't understand, Mr Rajput. I cannot face Dr Neerja.' Avik was insistent.

'What is the matter, Avik? You sound very disturbed,' Mr Rajput inquired.

'Remember I told you that someone shot me? Dr Neerja was behind it. I just overheard her speaking to Dr Tarun. She does not want Ananki to leave the NGO, as it would mean a great financial loss for her. For this she tried to have me killed. I am not going back to that NGO. Either you come and take Ananki or send a car for her. Do not tell Dr Neerja that you plan to take Ananki from the NGO forever; tell her it is only for a day or two, on Priyanka's wish.'

'Oh God! I can't believe Dr Neerja could stoop so low. I trusted her.' Mr Rajput was shocked at the revelation.

'We cannot know whom to trust, Mr Rajput.'

'I will call her immediately and ask her to send Ananki. But you will have to be with her once she is out of the building.'

'Okay, then send two cars to the NGO. Dr Neerja can escort Ananki to one, but the other car should remain out of sight. I will get into that car and follow Ananki for some distance before shifting into her car,' Avik suggested.

Dr Neeja tried her best to make Mr Rajput rethink his decision, but she had to give in to his wish. The plan worked. She made Ananki change into the clothes that the chauffeur had brought. She held her hand as they walked through the corridor.

'Take all your medicines on time. I will call Radha and tell her about them. Do not be stubborn, be back soon. I'll wait for you,' Dr Neerja told her as they walked out of the NGO.

'Don't worry, see you,' Ananki replied as she sat in the car that was waiting for her. Dr Neerja waved to her, biting her lower lip. She then dialled Avik's number to check where he was.

Avik did not pick up her call. Instead, he put his phone on silent mode. He was waiting in the second car parked at some distance from the main gate of the NGO, and asked the driver to follow Ananki's car as it pulled away. He could see the desperation on Dr Neerja's face through the tinted window of the car as it drove past her.

As per the plan, Avik shifted into Ananki's car after they were out of sight of the NGO. Distracted by the recent events, Avik failed to notice the strangeness in Ananki's attitude as she sat next to him in the rear seat. Ever since she had read the letter, all she had wanted was to confront her father, even if it meant being with Avik.

Avik slipped his fingers into hers. He felt he needed to reassure himself of her feelings for him. His future depended on how this relationship went forward. His breath was shallow as he leant his head against the window. There was a strain of fear underlying his nervousness.

Was it because Ananki could not be trusted or was it because he could not believe the kind of person he had become? Did he assume that being with Ananki would open the doors to Mr Rajput's wealth and status? Did he really want to spend his life with Ananki? What about love? Did he really love her?

Is love so important? Isn't love overrated? Not everyone finds the love of their life, their soulmate. Those that do find love lose it little by little every day, in the squabbles and skirmishes of everyday existence. Maybe love is not for me.

Ananki knew that something was wrong with Avik. She had never seen him so lost in his own thoughts. He appeared to her to be a prisoner of his mind.

People philosophize that our body is a cage while our mind stands free. It is gifted with the power of imagination to be wherever it wants to be, to do whatever it wants to do. But actually the mind is a trickster. It changes from being the limitless sky to a tiny cage within the blink of an eye. We do not believe it because we like to see the better, hope for the better, she thought, studying his face.

Avik's mind was like a wild horse that needed to be tamed. It rushed into decisions that should have been thought over a thousand times. He did not rein in his impulses. On the other hand, despite living in a mental institution, Ananki showed perfect control over hers. Her mind always knew what she wanted, and her body always acted according to it.

They were approaching the turn-off for her home, and when the chauffeur drove past it, Ananki became alarmed.

'Why did you not take the turn for Civil Lines?' she asked the driver. 'Take the next turn,' she instructed him.

'But Mr Rajput told me to take you to the house in Panchsheel,' Avik told her.

He turned to the driver. 'Take us to Panchsheel.'

Ananki was enraged. She dug her nails into Avik's wrist, leaving deep red marks. She hit him on his arms till he held her hands tightly. He tried to pacify her, but she threatened to jump out of the moving car if he did not tell the driver to take them home. Avik had no choice but to do as she told him to.

On reaching her home, she did not wait for Avik but ran straight inside. Mr Rajput was in the living room and stood up from the couch on seeing her rushing towards him. She stopped right in front of him, looked him in the eye and showed him the letter. Mr Rajput turned his face away and saw Avik entering the living room. Avik walked up to them and asked Ananki to come with him to her room.

'It has been a long ordeal for you, Ananki. You need rest. You can talk to your father later,' Avik said.

'Please stay out of this, Avik. It's none of your business,' she replied, pushing him away.

'Stay out of it? How can you expect me to stay out of it after all that has happened between us?' Avik grabbed her hand and attempted to pull her towards her room.

'Some things are extremely personal, Avik. This is something that is not related to you. I don't want you mixed up in it, you understand that,' Ananki said as she freed her hand and pushed him even harder, making him stumble onto the couch.

'Please leave,' she said in a shrill voice.

But Mr Rajput was not ready to face her alone. 'Please don't go, Avik,' he said, the desperation clear in his voice.

Avik nodded.

Ananki did not seem to be interested in Avik any longer. All she wanted was to find out the truth about the letter. She turned to Mr Rajput once again.

'I want to know if you really wrote this,' she asked.

He cleared his throat and replied after a pause, 'Yes. I wrote it.'

Ananki seemed offended by his answer, but she did not stop there.

'If I was really adopted, where are the adoption papers?'

Mr Rajput was prepared for this question, as was Avik. He looked at Mr Rajput who maintained his composure. Avik prayed for the success of their plan. All depended on whether Mr Rajput could allay Ananki's doubts.

'They were lost when we shifted from our previous home to this bungalow. I didn't want you to know that you were adopted, so I never bothered to get the papers reissued. However, after Kalki's death I tried to contact the adoption home and found out that they had closed down a long time ago due to lack of resources,' Mr Rajput replied.

Ananki seemed sceptical. She looked from Avik to her father and sat down on the couch. A range of expressions flashed across her face, as though she was speculating on Mr Rajput's story. Sometimes she bit her lower lip, sometimes she pursed her lips, at times her eyelids twitched and she rubbed her forehead with two of her fingers. Whether she believed it or not, one thing was for sure, the letter had affected her deeply and it showed in her body language.

Suddenly, Ananki jumped up from the couch and went straight to her room. The men looked at each other in bewilderment. Ananki returned within minutes. She carried a box in her hand. It was a small jewellery box, its surface covered in small mirrors of all shapes and sizes. It looked like a box made in an arts-and-crafts class from leftover mirrors. A tiny lock safeguarded its contents. Ananki placed the box in Mr Rajput's hands.

'Open it,' she told him in a mocking tone.

Mr Rajput looked closely at the box and the lock. He kept it on the table without saying a word.

'You cannot open it. Just like you could never open my heart and see what was in there for you. But you know what, I don't care now. I think I will settle for what I have found. But you should see what is inside it,' Ananki said.

She threw the box on the floor, shattering it into countless tiny mirrors that shimmered. Among them lay a diamond ring. It looked like a full moon amidst an infinite number of stars twinkling in the sky. Mr Rajput reached for it at once. His eyes were full of tears as he looked at it as if it was not just a ring but a memento of something very dear to him. The ring had belonged to Kalki. It was her wedding ring.

'How did you get hold of Kalki's ring? Was it not with her at the time of the accident? Did you steal it from her beforehand?' he cried in anger.

Ananki gave him a sly smile. 'Steal? You should be thankful that I pulled it off in time so that you can keep it in remembrance of her.'

'You pulled it off? You saved this ring, but you did not save her from that fatal accident?' Mr Rajput shouted with rage at Ananki.

'Accident? You still believe it was an accident?' Ananki guffawed.

'I know she killed herself because of you,' Mr Rajput shouted.

'Did she really kill herself?' Ananki burst out laughing as she said it.

The men were stunned.

'Mrs Rajput did not commit suicide?' Avik asked.

'No. She could not understand what had happened between Da and me. She wanted to teach me a lesson. Unfortunately, before she could, she died.'

Mr Rajput could not believe his ears. Although he had always maintained that his wife had died in an accident, all this while he had privately thought that Kalki had committed suicide because she thought her husband had betrayed her by sleeping with Ananki.

No matter how exasperated Mr Rajput was with Ananki for being the cause of his separation from Kalki and her subsequent death, he could not kill her with his own hands.

At the same time he did not want to see her ever again either. All he could do was make sure she never came back. But all did not go as he had wanted. There she was standing in front of him, looking right into his eyes and having the audacity to tell him that his wife had died because a mad girl did not want her to live.

'How could you?' he shouted.

'I had to kill her. She did not understand what I felt for you. She wanted to send me away from you. She wanted to live with you happily ever after. I made sure she failed. I killed her because if I had not, then she would have killed me. That was what she had planned when she took me in her car and sped onto the flyover. She wanted to throw me out of the car, straight into the Yamuna. When I realized what she wanted to do, I tried to stop her. We struggled in the car, which crashed into the barricade. The front of the car was hanging over the side of the bridge, but I managed to get out. Then I gave her my hand. She thought I was going to help her get out of the car. Instead I pulled the ring from her hand. I gave the car a kick. Within seconds the car became her coffin.' Ananki laughed loudly after narrating the account.

'How could you kill your mother? Did you not think even once about what you were doing before committing such a cardinal sin?' Mr Rajput howled.

'What sin? You told me in your letter that she was not my real mother. So that makes me a murderer, not a sinner.'

'Murder too is a sin, Ananki. When you killed her she was your mother by law,' Mr Rajput said.

'All I knew was that she was the wall that stood between you and me. You would never have loved me if she lived,' Ananki replied.

Mr Rajput could no longer hear the word 'love' from her. He went to her and slapped her hard across her face, making her fall to the floor. She looked up at him and smiled, making him all the more enraged. He grabbed her by the collar and pulled her up, then held her by the throat, increasing the pressure as she stood there in front of him. Avik rushed over to them and begged Mr Rajput to leave her, pulling at the hand that was trying to strangle her.

'Mr Rajput, no. Please calm down, for God's sake, calm down, leave her, please,' he pleaded.

'The wall still persists. It will always be present, no matter who lives and who dies. I can never love you, even though she is dead. I hate you and I will always hate you, till my last breath.' Mr Rajput pushed Ananki onto the couch and hurried out of the living room for some fresh air to calm his anger. He was afraid that the pent-up anguish within him might lead him to kill her.

Just as he opened the door of his car he heard a gunshot. He ran back inside the house to see if Avik was all right. He saw Ananki holding his gun. She knew the passcode of his safe. Radha and all the other servants came running to the living-room door but they could not dare to enter inside. Not one of them had the courage to rescue Avik from her wrath.

Avik was trying to calm her down. Mr Rajput knew she wouldn't listen to Avik, or even to him anymore. He wanted to snatch the gun out of her hand and kill himself. After all that he had seen happening before his eyes, he could only rest in death.

'Ananki, please stop. Hand the gun over to me right now,' Mr Rajput said, trying to take the gun from her.

'Yes, Ananki, listen to him, nothing can come of pointing a gun, I'm sure you know that very well,' Avik pleaded.

'Of course it can, Avik. Let me first tackle you so that you shut your mouth. What did you think? That I have feelings for you? Bullshit. All my life I have loved only one man, this one standing right in front of you. And after all these years of veneration, you thought I would fall for you? What in the world made you think that? Being a journalist, did you not study me well? You should have known. Anyway, I don't care because in your failure I succeeded. I succeeded in coming out of that dungeon and into his home. I will make him love me at any cost. And you, my dear, can leave now. I thank you for your services,' Ananki said, pointing the gun at Avik.

Avik was aghast. He felt like she had pillaged him and left him to suffer the aftermath. Never in his life had he felt more abused. Ananki had not only used him but also humiliated him by calling what he had done for her his 'services', as if he was nothing more than a harlot.

Although a part of him acknowledged that he had become a whore by letting Ananki use him, in return for which he had expected both position and wealth from Mr Rajput, he was also shaken because his plan had failed miserably.

He realized that all this while, it had been Ananki's stage and her play and he had become a secondary character, his part of the truth transmuted into a lie. It was time for him to make his exit because Ananki, the playwright, wished it so.

'Ananki, don't do this. You will not find another man like him. I like him too. He is the one for you,' Mr Rajput tried to convince Ananki to accept Avik's love, but she interrupted him.

'How can you even think that I would settle with any other man? It is either you or no one. Avik, leave us alone or I will shoot.'

'Avik, please don't leave. I cannot handle this alone,' Mr Rajput said, anxious to have his support in facing the hurricane that Ananki had become.

Ananki was furious to see the men banding together against her. She shot the huge vase placed close to where Avik was standing. Mr Rajput had no choice but to let him go.

'It's better that you go, Avik, I cannot withstand another murder in this house,' he said.

Avik nodded and moved towards the door. As he walked out, he felt something was pulling him back, as if his feet were tied to an anchor. The further he went from her, the greater the emptiness in him grew. He stopped when he could bear the vacuum in his spirit no more.

Why am I feeling this way? It can't be possible. Please. No. No matter how much he denied it, he suddenly realized that he had fallen in love with this madwoman.

What would I be without her? I don't think I can imagine a life in which I cannot see her. I have to try one last time, not for my dream but for the sense of completeness that this mad self has brought into my life.

He went back to her.

'Ananki, please listen to me,' Avik pleaded as he walked slowly towards her.

'Just go away,' Ananki shouted.

'You can shoot me if you want, but listen to what I have to say to you,' he said.

Ananki was not willing to listen to him. She was about to pull the trigger when Mr Rajput jumped in front of her.

'Listen to what he has to say, for the sake of the help he gave you,' Mr Rajput said.

'You have two minutes – say whatever you have to and leave,' she ordered him.

'I knew about your feelings for Mr Rajput, yet still I fell for you. I have never felt more alive in my life than in the past few weeks. What will you get from loving this man standing here? Nothing. He has never loved you, nor will he love you now, after I leave. You will remain as hollow as you have always been. Think about the void in your soul. He will never fill it. Why do you have to waste your life in pursuing the love of a man who does not love you in return? Why can you not accept the companionship of a man who is willing to stand by you as long as he lives?'

Avik had not finished when she shot him, hitting him just below his left knee.

'Leave,' she roared like a tigress ready to rip him apart.

Mr Rajput grabbed Avik before he fell to the floor. He held him and quickly dragged him to his car, asking his chauffeur to take him to the nearest hospital.

'I love her,' Avik told Mr Rajput as he sat inside the car. 'I really do.'

Mr Rajput did not know what to say, but his eyes were filled with emotion. He nodded without looking Avik in the eye.

'How will I explain this?' Avik asked him, pointing to the wound and changing the subject immediately.

'I will call Dr Anand. He is a dear friend. He will not report this unless you want him to,' Mr Rajput assured him.

'Okay, thank you,' Avik replied.

Mr Rajput made the call to Dr Anand, quickly explaining the situation, and then headed back to the living room with a determined gait. He approached Ananki.

'Stop or I will shoot,' she warned him.

'You can shoot. I have no wish to breathe for another moment,' he replied, his voice firm.

'I have loved you so much. Can you not return even one per cent of what I have always bestowed upon you?' she asked him, falling on her knees, pleading for his love but still holding the gun firmly in her hands.

'I loved you as a father loves his daughter, nothing more than that, but not less either,' Mr Rajput replied, standing in front of her.

'But I have loved you in every way possible and you will have to love me back, else you will see everyone that you love die an excruciating death,' she said.

He could not bear to hear any more. He snatched the gun from her hand, held it firmly and stood like a rock. Ananki was startled, but she had nothing to lose. She was not afraid to die. She smiled and crawled towards him to take back the gun.

Mr Rajput pointed the gun at himself and warned her not to come any nearer. He knew that only his death could affect her.

'It's better to shoot myself than be shot by you. A girl who can point a gun at her own father can do anything. Yes, I am your real father. The letter was devised to divert your madness away from me, but unfortunately it did not succeed,' Mr Rajput told her in desperation.

Ananki felt content upon hearing his words. There was not a barrier in this world, biological, social or cultural, that could stop her.

Mr Rajput cocked the gun. His death was the only way she would lose. She jumped up and ran towards him and pulled at the hand pointing the gun at his head.

The gun fired in the air. Seeing the tussle between the father and the daughter, Radha mustered courage to call the cops. Mr Rajput struggled to free his hand so he could pull the trigger again, but she would not let him. She bit him on his hand, causing him to release his hold on the gun, and she quickly took it from him.

Tears trickled down her cheeks at the thought of his death. Even though he could not understand her love, his life was more important to her than anything else.

She remembered the times when he would hold her in his arms whenever she fell down. Today she would fall down for the last time, never to get up again, but she was happy, since his arms would be holding her. She smiled at him and calmly shot herself in the head. She looked at him for the last time, as if capturing his image within her before her spirit left its cage. She saw him cry. She felt her body go numb and could not lift her hand up towards his face. She wanted to tell him to wipe away his tears and smile, but could not do so. The light from her stage faded out slowly. The play of her life had ended.

Epilogue

Dear Avik,

How have you been? It has been two months since I last saw you, on the day you were injured. After performing Ananki's funeral rites I went to the hospital to see you, but you had already left. Your mother answered your phone but would not let me talk to you. I called Dr Tarun, who told me that Dr Neerja had been arrested for being the one behind the attack on you. He gave me your friend Khyati's number. She refused to help me find you at first, but after assuring her that I meant you no harm she gave me your phone number in Mumbai. It was not reachable, however, so I had to go to your office in Mumbai, hoping I would find you there. Your boss told me you had resigned and shifted permanently to Delhi. He gave me your email address. He also told me about your failed attempt to uncover Ananki's story. He said it was the reason behind your resignation, despite him giving you a promotion.

You do not know how grateful I am to you. Like a real man, you kept your promise and did not share Ananki's story with Mr Sahay, in spite of all the perks that he offered. I also know that you are working for an NGO now and are earning a modest salary. Please, come and join my company. It will give me immense pleasure to have you on the team of my close associates. You have earned my trust and I want people like you to work for me.

Hope to see you soon.

R. Rajput.

Dear Mr Rajput,
How have you been? I am sorry for just vanishing. It's true that I kept my word and did not share her story. But in enacting all the drama that we had planned, I realized that I had really started to love her. She is dead for the world, for you too, but for me, she is present in my subconscious. No matter how hard I try to make her leave, I fail.

I thank you for your generous offer but at this point in time, I cannot accept it. I need more time to free my mind from her. I hope you will understand my circumstances. The day I am free from this obsession, I will call you. I still have your number.

Regards,
Avik

As Avik sent the email to Mr Rajput, he put his hand into his pocket and took out a piece of paper. He read again the poem Ananki had given him:

This prison of air, from which,
I can watch what goes out,
helplessly waiting to participate
in the games people play.
This infinite air constricting
what I see and feel, my being
chained with its endless spume
vapours of society cover me.
This abstruse cloak I wear
while moving amidst plasters
that can smell the negation
of endless vows of suppression.
Eternal self lost in this air
I seek one last time, once more.
Will I break free or the vacuum
of this byzantine prison, consume?

With wet eyes, he folded the paper, kept it back in his pocket and left for another world, an NGO that worked with mentally challenged children, a world that did not know the dualities of sane/insane, reason/madness, normal/abnormal. It was where Avik found not only happiness but also the love that he had lost.

Acknowledgements

This book would not have been conceived had I never studied Greek literature under Dr Abhishek Sharma, my guru, lecturer, Delhi University. His lectures challenged and changed my way of thinking and made me aspire for greater things in life. Thank you, sir, for guiding me throughout on both the professional and personal fronts.

If today I can hold this book in my hands, it is because of Ravinder Singh, my friend, book agent, inspiration and critic. His life stories have kept me going through my worst times.

I thank my publisher HarperCollins for deciding to publish this bold subject and my editor Prerna Gill who worked really hard with me to make this book what it is today.

My friend and the first reader of my book, Aditya Gupta, who read and reread my book several times. With every paragraph that he thought could be written better, I got better.

I cannot thank my life partner enough for supporting me and always doing a bit extra so that I could write. I know it wasn't easy with his job and a baby.

Lastly and most importantly, thank you Mom and Dad for raising me the way you have. If I am unstoppable today, it is because of both of you.